BLACK CANYON

All those who had robbed the train between Warbeck and Gaspard were now dead, including Jack Chandler, believed to be the only one who had known where the money was hidden. But someone else did know, and now, years later, waited for the chance to lift it. The gun-blazing outcome was centred on the killer, Nash, ruthless in his quest for the Chandler money and for personal revenge.

FRANK SCARMAN

BLACK CANYON

Complete and Unabridged

LINFORD
Leicester

First published in Great Britain in 1996 by
Robert Hale Limited
London

First Linford Edition
published 1997
by arrangement with
Robert Hale Limited
London

British Library CIP Data

Scarman, Frank
Black Canyon.—Large print ed.—
Linford western library
1. Western stories
2. Large type books
I. Title
823.9'14 [F]

ISBN 0-7089-5055-8

Published by
F. A. Thorpe (Publishing) Ltd.
Anstey, Leicestershire

Set by Words & Graphics Ltd.
Anstey, Leicestershire
Printed and bound in Great Britain by
T. J. Press (Padstow) Ltd., Padstow, Cornwall

This book is printed on acid-free paper

1

BASCOM, the watcher they had put in place, would now have to tell them that soon — within the next twenty minutes — they would have visitors.

Bascom had been sent to a position about halfway down on the left-hand side of this very rough ravine, well enough concealed but manifestly uncomfortable in the baking stillness of the day, and he had been wiping at his eyes and squinting hard at what he had become convinced were horses out there. His gleaming, pocked, whiskery face immobile, he was straining to focus, fighting the distortions of distance in order to be quite certain in his own mind about it before raising the alarm. The tiny images were parting, then merging again, but after a while Bascom came to the conclusion that there were at least two of them and they were heading unswervingly in his direction.

The small act of getting himself up out of his squatting position wrenched at Bascom's joints so that for a few seconds he was compelled to stand in a bent-over attitude, hands gripping his knees. "Jesus!" Presently he straightened and began making his way upward, working carefully among sharp-clawed brush, watching where he was placing his old boots as he went, and conscious that he must not betray any movements to whoever was coming.

Almost five minutes had passed before Bascom, breathing hard, mounted a jutting shelf of granite and once there paused, looking up, knowing they would still be there but not yet able to see any of them from where he was at the moment; so he cupped soiled hands to his stubbly mouth and called softly, "Nash?"

After a short interval a voice asked, "What?"

"Comp'ny."

Bascom's ear could now just catch the urgent muttering of conversation among men still unseen, then Nash's voice came again. "C'mon up."

Again Bascom began picking his laborious way up towards them, his breath rasping in his throat now, his brown shirt with the open, studded leather vest over it clinging to him; and he was dusty, tired, baggy-eyed under the shadow of his wide-brimmed, greasy hat. Bascom was about ready to spit iron now, because in his opinion they had been in this shit of a ravine for far too long, and for all their efforts they had found nothing except a couple of disgruntled rattlers. And now some other bastards were on their way in.

Before Bascom had quite arrived at the place where the others were, Nash, incomprehensibly, perhaps without thinking, asked, "Posse?"

"Real small bastard if it is," Bascom grunted. "Two hats, I reckon."

"More goddamn' prospectors," Nash

said, his thong-hanging grey hat shoved back, some of his thinning, light-coloured hair visible.

There were two others besides Nash, in unkempt, dusty clothes. All of their horses had been kept well out of view nearer the upper reaches of this ravine and in the shade of overhanging rock.

There was a heavy-set man named Brophy, with black, alert eyes in a wide face, and a middle-aged, bony man called Staples who, at this moment had taken off his raggy, red bandanna and was wiping his coarse, lined face with it. The removal of the bandanna had revealed an ugly stripe across the left side of Staples' stringy neck, a mark that looked what it was, an old but fierce rope-burn that had refused to fade with time, part of Staples' history of near-death, branded on him for life. Now retying the bandanna, Staples said, "I'll go on up an' wait with the mounts, make damn' sure they stay quiet."

Nash nodded, then said to Bascom

and Brophy, "Best yuh git in behind some brush down there, close enough so yuh kin cover me."

"Yuh goin' on down?" Bascom asked.

"Not all the way," said Nash, "but I want to git me a real early look at these bastards. Jes' make sure nothin' shines."

When the distant images clarified, emerging gradually from out of the heat-haze, it could be perceived that Bascom had been only partly correct; indeed there were two horses, but it turned out that what they had here was one mounted man with a pack-horse in tow.

Having come to that conclusion, Nash settled himself down to wait, concentrating his attention on the approaching rider but thinking ahead, too, realizing that if this man was indeed heading for this particular ravine, then because of outcrops of rock further down there must come a point at which he would pass from

Nash's sight, then reappear only when he was into the ravine itself. That would be a critical time, Nash thought, for the man would appear suddenly, and much closer, and although access to this often brush-choked, jagged place was not easy, it was by no means impossible, even for a man leading a pack-horse, provided he proceeded with care.

This was the place, this bad ravine, where in the past a posse out of Warbeck had cornered and then taken the notorious Jack Chandler, and this although Chandler had been among rocks and above them at the time, so in Nash's opinion they had been goddamn' lucky to get it done and only one dead. Anyway, that was all history now, and as it turned out there had been a lot more dead before that particular episode was all over.

Inexorably the rider was bobbing onwards and there was seen to be about him a slump that told of many hot miles at his back, yet he was coming with a purposeful set to him, his objective now plainly within his view.

Mounted on what appeared to be a strongly-muscled bay horse, he was a man who could now be seen to have on a red-and-white-chequered shirt, moleskin pants and a tall-crowned, wide-brimmed hat; and the pack-horse he was leading seemed to be quite generously loaded, and with what was perhaps a shovel handle and a pick handle sticking out back from the general baggage.

The man who was waiting and watching in the ravine was now seeking evidence of a scabbarded rifle but could not find one. From above there came a slight skittering of small stones and Nash's head snapped around in annoyance before he brought his attention back to the man with the pack-horse. Nash's dark-grey shirt was clinging to him, darker sweat-patches all over it, and his hat bore a rim of sweat on sweat. In the cooler morning he had started out wearing a canvas brush-jacket but as the close, rising heat had enveloped them he had been compelled to discard it and take his chances on being raked.

One agreeable thing about the present pause in proceedings was that it was offering Nash an opportunity to think matters over without having to respond to a string of unanswerable questions from Brophy and Staples and Bascom, mainly because things had not been going as well as they had hoped. Indeed, it was only just beginning to occur to some of them that maybe somebody might have got here ahead of them and located the money; but Nash himself, although he had considered it, could not truly accept that, not being able to bring himself to believe that if some bastard *had* had the good luck to stumble on it there would have emerged to the wider world not so much as one whisper of it. Something would have come to him.

Even as these thoughts were going

through Nash's mind, the rider and his pack-animal, in their unflagging advance, were as he had anticipated passing from his line of vision. Waiting, trying to suppress his impatience, Nash grasped the warm, hardwood butt of the Smith and Wesson Army, lifted the weapon from its old holster and slipped the latch to open the pistol, checking the five bright loads in the cylinder; then with a solid click he closed it again. He slid the Smith and Wesson back down in its holster, again feeling the weight of it resting against his thigh.

After an interval it did occur to Nash that whoever this newcomer was, he might have chosen not to enter the ravine at all but had changed direction abruptly or had dismounted for some purpose.

Nash was in fact on the point of giving up and making his way back up to where Brophy and Bascom were when some sounds from below caused him to hesitate, and he then stood watching as the chequerboard-shirted horseman, the pack-animal still trailing him, came around a slab of granite down on the narrow floor of the ravine and began making his tortuous way upwards. At this much closer proximity shovel and pick handles could clearly be seen within the jumble of equipment being carried by the second horse. Prospector indeed, Nash thought, but quite well aware of the mother-lode that was to be sought here.

Nash now fought to control his impatience, waiting until the mounted man drew even closer, below him; but rather sooner than he would have preferred, the horseman — a broad-shouldered, brown-bearded man he was — abruptly drew rein and spoke to both horses, which stood, heads hanging, in the trapped heat of this rocky, unkempt place, as another rattle of small stones came from somwhere above.

That left Nash with no option. He stood up.

The man below, his bushy face

shadowed under his wide-brimmed hat, looked up in astonishment and his mouth fell open. "Jesus!"

"Yep, back from the dead," said Nash who could now perceive that the man sitting the bay had on old, faded clothing but which was in reasonably good repair, and that his boots were old, too, but had been well made. If he was truly a prospector, then by the general appearance of him he was an unusually fastidious one. The horse was indeed a strong animal, the pack-animal certainly no dog; and the equipment looked to be well preserved. There appeared to be no armaments whatsoever. None visible, of course, did not mean that there were none.

"An' who might you be, mister?"

"Ulrich," the horseman said, "an' I might ask the same."

"Yuh might at that," said Nash.

The shadowed eyes of the mounted man were now probing beyond and above Nash but there was neither sound nor movement anywhere, as though he and the ugly, armed man standing ahove him might be the only life within a hundred miles. Ulrich must have been aware, however, that such was not the case. Equally, he must have known that the hard-eyed man who had materialized out of the dusty rocks had every advantage, and that there had come and gone a tick of time in which he, Ulrich, had had his fate sealed. Perhaps for an instant he had glimpsed it in the agate eyes of the other man or in some way had witnessed a strange shadow flit between them, one that lacked substance to cause it. Sweat was running between Ulrich's shoulder-blades and his broad hands were greasy with it, but it was sweat that was death-cold. Above him the man stood watching as though actually capable of following the thoughts that were hastening through Ulrich's mind, for when at last Ulrich evaluated his chances of either getting off the horse fast and into some sort of cover, or turning both the bay and the pack-horse in that confined passage and retreating, Nash suddenly said, though quietly, "Yuh'd never git it even half done, mister."

But, against the odds, Ulrich did try. Because turning both of the horses was manifestly out of the question, he chose to get himself down out of the saddle as fast as he could, with the object of placing the animal's bulk between himself and the man above him, though to what further gain was unclear. Perhaps it was simply the natural reaction of a man who has realized that what had started out as a menacing stand-off was about to turn into gunfire.

Ulrich's right leg was swinging back over the cantle when Nash, his right shoulder in a dipping motion, drew the Army and without undue hurry, lifting it, blasted at Ulrich and hit him hard in the right breast, pounding him further around so that, his left boot still in the stirrup, Ulrich seemed to be performing a wild pirouette high up on the horse; then as Nash, hazed in gunsmoke, shot again, he was flung backwards, coming free of the stirrup, to go crashing down among unyielding stones, the bay horse now lunging and tugging at the pack-animal which was attached by a long leather thong to the saddlehorn of the bay.

At the sound of the sudden shooting that went climbing in whacking echoes up the ravine, Brophy and Bascom, higher up, came into view.

Nash, his gun still drawn, steadying himself with his outstretched left hand, had begun making his way down towards the horses, small stones disturbed by his descent running with a rattling noise ahead of him.

The bay was tossing its head and blowing and Nash paused to catch hold of it and steady it, then walked on, crunching over loose stones to where the bearded man lay, life shuddering out of his broad body even as Nash's long shadow fell across him. Nash bent forward to look, then straightened, glancing behind him to see Brophy and Branscom making their way down between branches of brush.

"Nailed 'im?" Brophy called.

"Yep," said Nash.

By the time they reached him, both sweating profusely, Bascom wiping at his own face with a crooked arm, Nash was finishing a closer inspection of the dead man.

"Know 'im?" asked Boscom.

"Nope. Said his handle was Ulrich." Then, "He's got to be the fussiest goddamn' prospector I ever did run across." It was certainly true that, even bloodied as they now were, Ulrich's shirt and pants were very well preserved, as were his boots; and in fact, as Nash had felt a little earlier, everything the man had with him was of a certain quality, and it marked him out as a cut above what he appeared to be.

Nash, having slid the pistol away, squatted down, and as they looked on, went through all of the dead man's pockets, finding only a few small bills and some coins, a stubby, blackened pipe and a part sack of tobacco. When, a short time later, they sorted through all of the stuff on the pack-horse, they discovered nothing of particular interest, and neither of the horses bore a brand of any kind.

Finally Nash, looking down at the body of the bearded man, shoved at its sodden weight with the toe of one boot as though to stir from it some kind of confession.

"Too good to be true, this bastard," he said. He added that he now wished that he had kept the prick alive long enough to ask him a few questions. Too late for that now. Nash stepped across to the heap of belongings, selected the pick-axe and tossed it to Brophy. "Brought all the necessary tools along, anyway," he said. "Let's git some ground broke an' git him in a hole."

Sourly Brophy looked at Nash but began casting about for a likely spot.

Bascom asked, "What we gonna do with these here animals?"

"Be glad they've come our way," said Nash, "them an' all this stuff here."

Brophy suggested that Bascom take up the shovel and give him some help.

2

THE substantial town of Gaspard, bisected by glinting railroad tracks, had an impressive depot and a multi-tracked freight-yard. It was a place of commerce, Gaspard, the hub of Delmar County, a conglomeration of barns, corrals, stores, saloons and houses, a red-brick town hall which dominated the junction of three streets, a county courthouse with a tall flagpole, and a jailhouse where also was to be found the office of the Delmar County sheriff, Ed Macken, and his three deputies, Collis, Sloane and Reece.

Gaspard lay well to the south-west of the smaller town of Warbeck in Slane County, which in turn was to the west of Fayette; and Gaspard was close in to the pine- and fir-clothed Fayette Hills, and by late afternoon the shadows of those hills and of the mountains behind them, the High Torres, reached out across it.

Macken stood now with his calloused hands on his hips, looking along the length of a busy main street that bristled on either side with signboards of every description: dry-goods, attorney, dentist, barber, printer, bank, saloon, hotel, Wells Fargo, mercantile and a host of others.

Macken, however, was looking at none of these nor any of the people criss-crossing the street. He had eyes only for a pair of raggy-looking men who he was well aware stank of old sweat and new whiskey and who had been in an argument with a bar-dog up at a saloon called the Red Deuce. At the crucial moment Macken had strolled in and told them to back off and to get on their way.

The round-faced deputy, Collis, thumbs hooked in his belt, came unhurriedly along the boardwalk and stopped near Macken.

"Who are them pricks?"

"Just what yuh said," said Macken. "I give 'em the hard word an' now they're leavin'."

They stood observing as the two horses, short-reined, went shuffling away from the tie-rail and were then hauled around to go moving up Main towards the farther end and eventually out of town. Neither Macken nor Collis stopped watching them, however, until it became quite certain that the pair of bobbing horsemen really were on their way out. Another minor, yet annoying and unpleasant task behind him, Macken, accompanied by Collis, made his way back to his office fronting the county jail.

The men he had just sent on their way were of a sort that had become all too common around Gaspard, particularly since the robbery of the South-Western railroad freight about halfway between Gaspard and Warbeck, just across the Slane County line, and the subsequent concealing by a bandit named Jack Chandler of the sacks of money taken from the express-car. Dead now, Chandler was, his secret gone with him to the grave, so it was said, yet a cloying uncertainty about that had been the powerful magnet which since that time had drawn men of all stripes to the Fayette Hills region, and in particular to a bad ravine, the one in which Chandler had been challenged and taken while on his way out, by a posse out of Warbeck.

As they stepped inside the office, Collis trailing Macken, another deputy seated at an old desk, a small, stringy-necked man of forty, Bob Sloane, glanced up from his paperwork.

"Git shut of 'em?"

"Yeah," Macken said. "Piss-whiskered nobodies."

"They been up there to that ravine, scratchin' around?"

"Hard to tell," Macken said. "Didn't have no paraphernalia, an' they had but one pistol between 'em that to me looked dangerous to the user." Then,

"Where's Artie?" Artie Reece, the third deputy.

"Out to Lem Carrick's. Talk about the Sabre Creek claim."

Macken nodded. Dead land, unclaimed, except now by the county itself; and Carrick, a rancher, wanting to question it. The kind of thing which could easily turn into another ragged argument. "Artie been down to the county land office?"

"Yeah. Oh yeah."

Again Macken nodded, but had no conscience about having asked the question. Never assume anything was Macken's usual style. Well, it was all part and parcel of the county's law functions in a busy place such as this one, a place which could well do without having to deal with stinking, bad-mouthed itinerants. Anyway, it now had two fewer of those.

As though reading Macken's thoughts, scraping his chair, getting up to wander away to make coffee, Sloane said, "They do reckon Bob Gowan's still got that train money business stuck right up his ass."

"Yeah, I'd heard that." Macken as a matter of fact had plenty of other thoughts about Chandler's train money, but for the moment he chose not to debate that particular matter. Nothing would be done in a rush but there were things which might well have to be settled, not in Warbeck and not in the much-discussed ravine in the Fayettes, but right here in Gaspard. Now he pulled an age-worn watch from a pocket of his vest, snapped it open with a gnarled thumbnail, shut it and put it away. To Collis he said, "Time yuh was gone."

Collis, his plump face blank, nodded and left the office, his stint of duty at an end at least until early evening. Both Macken and the sharp-featured Sloane, now fetching in two steaming cups of coffee, watched Collis go out onto the boardwalk, turn left and pass from view.

Macken took up a mug and began

sipping, pacing around. Collis, he knew — as indeed would Sloane — would be heading on up to the Red Deuce, there to sit in on a game. In that place a dealer by the name of Stace Culley had developed an easy-going friendship with Deputy Collis, and as far as Macken was concerned, Collis would do well to watch his step, being a man who had gained no great reputation in the matter of faro, and Macken was conservative enough to be wary of awkward situations which might arise, especially those likely to compromise any of the county deputies in his charge. On the other hand it could be argued that what a man did in his own time was entirely his own affair, provided it was lawful, and Macken therefore knew that he had to tread carefully in those regions. Now he let these thoughts go and turned his attention to other things, while knowing that the Collis doubts would return to niggle at him again before long. Maybe it was not Collis at all that was troubling him though. Maybe it was Stace Cully.

Sloane, however, who Macken knew had developed something of a fixation about the robbery of the South-Western and its mysterious aftermath — for he had listened to a good deal that the railroad people in Gaspard had had to say about it — was unwilling to allow that subject to drop.

"I still don't understand," Sloane said, his Adam's apple bobbing in his stringy throat, "how it is nobody's come up with that money. Christ knows, for a good long while them hills was crawlin', folks pokin' around like ants in honey."

It was an old, well-worn subject, but Macken, his leathery face impassive, still sipping coffee, still pacing around aimlessly, sometimes pausing to stare through the grimy window at nothing in particular, could only come back to his own repeatedly-expressed views on the matter.

"I've said it before, as I see it there's

two possibilities: the sacks are still where Chandler put 'em or they've been found, an' whoever it was got 'em then got out without nobody else twiggin' it. Somebody on his own, no other mouths to open."

Because Sloane looked as though he did not want to accept that somebody had already got the money without at least him knowing about it, he said, "I know what that damn' place is like, the ravine, the lie o' the land all around. The money could be up a goddamn' tree fer all we know, but which one o' the ten thousand? Take your pick." Then, "Ol' Jack, he knew, but by all accounts he wasn't sayin'. Jack Chandler. Fancy him bein' dead, anyway. Well, he's sure enough left a blind guessin'-game behind him."

Macken chose not to comment further on it. A naturally cautious man and a thoughtful one when not unduly pressed by the numerous affairs that sometimes had to be dealt with in this office, he had begun to have some private doubts about the likes of Sloane's last remark. Macken finished his coffee and went clumping off to rinse the empty mug, having firmly decided that at least for the present he would say nothing of it to Sloane or anybody else.

Though Macken did not know it for sure, though strongly suspected it, others had come to the same half-conclusion that he had, and quite soon now that burgeoning feeling would serve to bring the whole sorry affair of the South-Western freight to a head. And had he known, Macken would not have fancied the outcome, with all its attendant hazards, one bit.

★ ★ ★

They had managed to get Ulrich buried. No, not buried, as such, mostly they had got him covered with stones, because down where he was even the pick-axe could not make a ready impression in this kind of ground. Then there had been a further discussion on what was to be done with Ulrich's horses. Bascom thought that if they took them along with them, the animals might be recognized.

"We don't know how far he come."

All of them were together now, Staples having come down from watching over the horses, their clothing sodden with sweat, all swatting angrily at flies. Nash said, "I told yuh once already, we'll take these here animals along with us when we go."

Bascom did not press the point but he did not look happy about it.

Now Staples spoke up. "We got to git more supplies from somewhere, an' soon, an' by Gawd I got a thirst on me fit to drain a goddamn' saloon." He fastened his yellowy eyes on Nash. "Where's it gonna be, Nashie, Warbeck or Gaspard? Or Fayette?"

"Gaspard," Nash said at once, and that seemed to confirm that he had been thinking about it.

"Warbeck's a mite closer," said

Brophy, his round face ruddy and sweat-slick. Boiled, he looked, Brophy.

"An' a sight smaller," said Nash, "where us an' all this rig would stand out like preachers in a whorehouse." While that was true enough, they did wonder, too, if Nash might have some natural reluctance to go riding into a town where, trying to break Jack Chandler out of the Slane County jail, riding with Ord Chandler and a man named Pearce, Nash's elder brother had been shot off his horse, by whom was unclear, some said the county sheriff, a man named Gowan, others said one of his deputies. Anyway, it did not much matter, the fact was that Nash's brother had died there in the main street of Warbeck in a raid that had been badly conceived and duly bungled; and between then and when it was all over, there had been four dead as well as Nash, one of those a Slane County deputy named Telfer who, incomprehensibly, had been persuaded to throw in with

Jack Chandler and had let him out of the cage, and that had turned out to be another bad blunder.

The upshot of all those activities had been a bad-tempered reaction from both the South-Western railroad and the US Treasury whose assigned marshals had put in an appearance shortly after, come with the expectation of taking the infamous Jack Chandler away with them for formal prosecution and eventually, it had been assumed, a rope. And it had meant, too an increase in the Slane County law establishment, so that as well as Gowan there were now two permanent deputies. A number of sharp lessons, or so it was said, had been learned over it all, particularly the break-out at Warbeck as it had become known, albeit not quite accurately, and it might reasonably be assumed that any strange faces turning up there were still being carefully looked over.

The brother of the dead Nash, along with Brophy, Staples and Bascom, were now assembled out beyond the jagged mouth of the ravine, mounted, grimy and tired, with Ulrich's bay horse minus its saddle and bed-roll, which had been concealed in the brush, and his pack-animal again laden. The party was at last about ready to set out for the town of Gaspard. Nash had pre-empted any further talk about their newly-acquired horses by saying, "The bay'll likely fetch a good price in town. The other'll come in useful when we start our own prospectin' again."

"Yuh mean to say we're comin' all the way back here to start over?" This was Staples.

"That's what I do mean," Nash said. "Yuh don't fancy that, git gone now." Staples shut up. Nash said, "There's all sorts o' word been blowin' about on the wind. Could be we'll spend a little time in Gaspard an' do some more listenin'."

Brophy, his flushed face sagging with weariness, did say however, "There's a real fine whorehouse in Gaspard, that I do know. Maggie Otis's."

"Oh Christ," said Bascom flatly. "All that means is they'll remember yuh. Mebbe some o' them doves in that place has still got the marks."

Nash looked sourly at both of them and reined his dusty chestnut horse away, Brophy and Bascome, exchanging grins and raised eyebrows, following him, then Staples, unwillingly leading Ulrich's pack-horse.

They did not know it yet but they were now heading towards interesting times in Gaspard and there would be set in motion in that town a train of events which would culminate in terror and violence.

3

THE howl of the circular saws driven by steam donkey-engines could be heard all over Gaspard. It was a sound inseparable from the town.

Malpass's lumber storage yard, on a backstreet, was a bustling enterprise, a place filled with the sounds of men and horses and wagons and the heavy pulsing of the engines driving the belts and flywheels and pulleys, lifting and hauling and sawing lumber; and the air was heavy with smells of steam, hot oil and sap-wet wood, the entire yard awash with sawdust.

This big workplace where sawn lumber was stockpiled and eventually shipped out from a railroad siding was one of two such sites operated by Arne Malpass, the other a few miles away under the shadows of the timber-slopes themselves, and from a spur-line there, he shipped out sawn timber as well as unsawn logs. Flat-deck wagons hauled other prime logs into Gaspard to the town mill where Malpass's main workforce was lodged in his company houses, and where this long store-yard lay, the whitish lumber, much of it under poled awnings, drying and maturing.

The man himself, Malpass, his large, unhealthy face expressionless as he walked around giving out instructions, making his presence felt, was a bulky, humourless individual and not one to cross if you happened to be on his payroll; except, that is, if you were Allie Joubert.

She was standing now at the grimy window of the yard office looking out at Malpass and hoping that he would continue to be fully occupied in yard affairs until it came time for her to quit for the day, so that she need have no further contact with him until tomorrow.

Allie had been working for Malpass almost from the time she had arrived in Gaspard from Warbeck. Malpass, the man of business and influence; and of the dowdy wife, Hetty; the man of the bad breath and the habit of standing too close when he talked. He tended to hang around the office watching Allie's every move, but so far — though she was certain it had been only with the utmost difficulty — he had managed to keep his hands off her. But he sure was sweating for her, was Malpass, everlastingly devouring her with his marbly eyes, perhaps imagining her with her customarily coiled-up brown hair loose and probably falling as far as her apple-tight bottom.

Hetty Malpass knew what was in his mind, too, for some days, on some pretext, she made it her business to call in at the office, and her small black eyes in her spongy face always went scything through Allie like reaphooks, while Malpass himself would be hovering in the background looking cowed, certainly much discomfited.

Allie virtually ran the town office. She dealt with buyers who came in, she attended to the accounts and she made up and paid the men's wages; and for what Malpass was paying her to do it, he knew he was on the winning end of the deal. But of course, she was too striking, too attractive. Forty now, Allie Joubert, but still with the cream-smooth skin of a woman fifteen years younger, the only wrinkles at the corners of her large, almond eyes. And her figure was neat and rounded, with a firm, girlish look to it; even though, when she first came to Gaspard, her clothing — though in good repair — had been shabby, every man who passed her had turned to look at her again. Now, with regular money coming in, such as it was, she had managed to buy herself some new clothes, not by any means flamboyant ones, but all of them most becoming, clothes which celebrated the lissome shape of her body.

Coming away from the window Allie took up a sheaf of papers and went to the wooden file-cabinet in one corner of the dingy office and began slipping them away; but her thoughts were ranging far beyond this mundane task, for behind her calm, retiring demeanour — which some were inclined to see as aloofness — was an alert mind, and it was the mind of a woman secure in the knowledge that she possessed vital information, information held by no-one else alive. Allie Joubert knew where Jack Chandler's train money was, the proceeds from a robbery that had been attended by a number of savage killings and which, at the time, had caused a real stir for hundreds of miles around.

Armed with leaked information, they had hit a South-Western freight, the Chandler brothers, Jack and Ord, Allie's own man, Stagg, and a fat, brutal man named Pearce, a train that was also hauling the anonymous olive-drab boxcar that turned out to be an express-car containing a substantial amount of Treasury money, in banded bills, not in a safe but guarded by marshals.

They got the train stopped a few miles out of Warbeck, not far beyond a spot called Yellow Face, and got the job of lifting the money done in double-quick time; but in the course of it they lost Stagg, who had been causing a lot of damage with a repeating carbine. But then, in the aftermath of the train, matters had not continued to run their way. Ord Chandler and the fat man, Pearce, had finished up on the one horse, Pearce's having gone lame, and Jack Chandler, in the belief that they might all stand a better chance of getting clear if he jettisoned the filled sacks, had gone off alone to stash them; but on the way out from doing that he had been a mite careless and had got himself pinned down by a posse out of Warbeck, led by Bob Gowan, trapped in fact in a rough ravine in the Fayette Hills below the High Torres and located between Warbeck and Gaspard.

So Jack Chandler, his shells all spent, had been taken to the county jail in Warbeck, there to await the arrival of US marshals, and by force of circumstance, the only man who knew where the money from the train was.

Predictably, Ord Chandler, Pearce and another man named Nash arrived to break Jack Chandler out, but because they had formed no detailed plan to do it, failed abysmally, Ord Chandler and Nash shot to bloody rags on the main street of Warbeck, and only fat Pearce away clear and free to make another try, for Jack Chandler's knowledge was the most powerful of drawcards.

Jack had managed to get out in the finish, though not because of Pearce's clumsy efforts, for by that time Gowan had trapped and nailed Pearce, but by the unlikely hand of one Augie Telfer, the Slane county deputy.

But as it had transpired, getting out of the Warbeck cage had been the only good luck that Jack Chandler had enjoyed, and even that had been a pleasure of brief duration.

Allie closed the drawer of the file-cabinet and went wandering pensively back to the yard window. Jack Chandler. The scene, the final scene, returned to her as she stood now, her slim arms folded, watching but scarcely seeing the unappealing Malpass moving around in the busy yard.

Laid out across three butted-together tables in Kelly's saloon in Warbeck was Jack Chandler, but there had been nothing at all that the doctor, Groves, could do for him at that stage. So while Allie herself sponged Chandler's forehead, all who were there simply waited uncomfortably for the end to come, Allie, Groves, the preacher Crowder, the owner Kelly, and Gowan, all in that dimly-lit, liquor-smelling place that still smelled, too, of burnt powder, and with shadows lurching across the walls and ceiling, Allie occasionally leaning closely over Chandler as he came to

40

partial awareness, whispering, only for him to go sliding away from her again, eyes closing. Three or four times he did that, came to himself, then went drifting off again, until at last he slipped from consciousness one more time, and that time he did not return.

Groves had then come forward to attend to last things and Crowder's lightweight, sing-song voice had started up, sounding eerily in the gloom: "*We humbly commend the soul of this thy servant our dear brother into thy hands* . . . " And the money, taken at such cost from the South-Western freight, into nobody's hands, at least not so far.

In the beginning, in going to Warbeck that time, her connection with the bandits not known, Allie had thought to claim only Stagg's share. Now there was nobody left alive except her, neither of the Chandlers, no Pearce, no Nash; and her own man, Stagg, had been one of the first to go. Poor old Staggie. He had had the appearance of some prissy banker but had frequently behaved like a whiskey-mad Apache.

Allie was very much on her own though, and she realized only too well that the knowledge she had acquired could well turn out to be lethal. She was, too, a woman in a raw and dangerous land and it was chiefly for this reason that she was still here in Gaspard, still trying to work out some relatively safe way to get to where the money was and then get out again with it and quietly fade away. That of course meant getting hold of a sound saddler and a good pack-horse as well, and the freedom to move without attracting undue interest, for she was by no means prepared to sacrifice everything at this point through some act of crass carelessness. Not for the first time she thought that what she needed was an ally. If she did, she did not yet know whether or not that person would turn out to be a man named Stace Culley. Somehow her relationship with him had developed well beyond her intentions, and to an extent against her better judgement. Allie was still being quite careful about what she said, even to Culley.

A tall, slim, handsome man, he was ten years younger than Allie. Always immaculately dressed, often in a light-grey suit, ruffled white shirt and blue string-tie, Culley dealt faro at the Red Deuce saloon and, so he said, had irons in various fires elsewhere; for he had not been in Gaspard even as long as had Allie herself. "Can't settle," he had told her. "Never could." One thing though, he never seemed to lack for money.

Allie glanced at the old wall-clock, its Roman numerals showing through smeared, dusty glass, and began putting things away into drawers and lastly locked the iron safe. She felt relieved. Time to go.

The yard door opened and Malpass came in, his narrow-brimmed hat set quite straight on his dome of a head. Allie had been about to drop the key to the safe into a drawer of his desk, but seeing it in her hand, he came across to take it from her. An opportunity to be close to her. Malpass smelled of the yard, the wood-smell, the oil and steam, and she turned her head slightly to avoid his breath.

"Time to go, I see," said Malpass.

Allie nodded, turning away, and was aware that as she moved towards the small side-table to pick up her hat and other belongings, Malpass, close behind her, had moved too. She made herself take the hat and settle it on her head, and at a small, specked wall-mirror, she could see him standing only a couple of feet from her back, watching her, drinking her in. She could feel warm dampness on her neck but fought to control her movements, taking up gloves and a small, beaded reticule, and then she turned towards the door. And Malpass, sweat dampening his jowls, did not move from her path.

The street door opened, and in some consternation Malpass half turned.

Stace Culley, a slightly lop-sided smile on his face under his dove-grey hat, nodded easily at Malpass, then flicked his glance to Allie.

"Seems I'm just in time."

"Just about to leave," said Allie levelly, her usually faint Southern accent seeming slightly more pronounced as sometimes it did if she was disturbed.

Malpass stood aside and Allie crossed the room and went out, Culley following her. Outside, he said, "A problem?"

Allie drew in a reaching breath, feeling ridiculously faint. "Could be. Maybe."

"From what I saw he looked fit to eat you," said Culley, "and then fit to eat *me* for a wholly different reason."

"Nothing's happened, not yet," she said.

"You need me to have a word? Say, and I will."

Without hesitation she shook her head. "If it does get to be a problem, then it will be my problem and I'll have to deal with it at the time." All at once she felt churlish at giving him that kind of answer but he appeared to take no offence, perhaps having accepted it as another manifestation of her independent spirit. But she did say, "Sometimes this town seems to close in on me, Stace, as though its next move might be to smother me altogether." She placed gloved fingers briefly against one temple. "Oh, I know I'm being stupid. It's just that Arne Malpass makes me feel jittery, and a man like that shouldn't be able to. I ought to be able to handle him better; but I do need the work, and work isn't easy to come by." She grinned at him. "Stace, there are times I'd like to be able to get out of this place for a while, even for a few hours."

"Why not do it, then? I could hire us a buggy."

"That would be real nice, Stace. Or horses. We could go riding. I *can* ride, you know. I used to, quite often, back home when I was a girl. Yes, now that would be nice."

Culley said again, "Why not?" Then, "Do you have riding-clothes?"

"Not yet — but right now my purse could just about run to a divided skirt."

"Then it's a deal."

They walked on, and after they had gone by, Ed Macken stepped to the doorway of his office and his hard eyes followed the pair of them until they went out of his sight.

4

THE two men wore city suits. They were in a sparsely-furnished room at the back of the substantial South-Western railroad building in Gaspard, Meares the S-W head man in this region, a bulky, balding individual, and the other a soberly-dressed man, tall, spare, with a long cadaverous face, slightly jowly in a middle-aged way, and who had dark hair streaked with grey, combed thickly back across his scalp.

Though it was evening only one lamp had been turned up in this room, a place which was not much more than an orderly storeroom, for the taller man, Dillon, had been concerned not to advertise their presence here at this hour, and Meares had complied readily enough, for the situation as far as he was concerned was one of some sensitivity now that this man had put in an appearance, counselling confidentiality.

"It is not merely a matter of the money," Dillon had insisted in his velvet voice (and Meares, staring at him lugubriously, had at first thought, but failed to find that it was said in a spirit of levity). "There is also a principle at stake here, a question of credibility. The wilder element must never be permitted to gain the impression that we take such things lightly or that we too readily abandon our interest in them. That would send out the wrong message entirely."

To a degree defensively, Meares said, "South-Western, as the carrier, always did take it seriously; and we lost five of our employees, an engineer, a fireman, a freight-conductor and two brakies; all shot down — by God, some of them were *put* down, no less — but there has to come a time when you have to look at the *point* of going on. After all, we did have some of our own people up there, all around those hills and all down that ravine where everybody seems to think the money was put, and they all came up empty-handed. Finally, word came down from Chicago. *Enough.* Unless we can get hold of some more information, there's no use in going on. That's my view."

"Oh, I do see that," said Dillon at once. "Far be it from me to suggest otherwise, but I have to tell you that we might just be close to the first real break in this entire business. I should know quite soon."

Meares nodded soberly, apparently mollified, for at first he had definitely been ruffled, and now he took out a silver pocket-watch. "He's taking his time."

"He has to take care, if anything is going to come of it," said Dillon. "Too many ears, too many prying eyes."

Meares nodded again, put his watch away and now took out a black cheroot and lit it, the sweet-smelling smoke at once evident in the confines of this small room. There came a tapping at the door and Meares moved across to open it.

Stace Culley came in and Meares, after a quick glance outside, shut the door behind him. Culley removed his light-grey hat, looked around for somewhere to hang it, found nothing, so stood with it in his hand.

"I'd have got here sooner," he said, sensing by his manner that Meares in particular had been getting impatient, "but there were a lot of people around and I wasn't prepared to take chances."

"Understood," said Dillon. "Well, any word for us?"

"No," said Culley, "nothing cut and dried, but maybe it's too soon to expect it." There was more that he might have said and did not, but Dillon's bloodhound eyes had been reading him.

"You also believe it's a waste of time, that man going up into the ravine?"

"I do," Culley said. "I could well

51

be right on the verge of getting other information."

Meares was studying Culley closely. It was Dillon, though, who said, "Mrs Joubert. I expect you mean from Mrs Joubert."

"Yes."

Dillon, his long-fingered hands clasped behind him, went pacing up the room — which meant a mere half-dozen steps — turned and came back.

Meares, looking slightly bemused now, not over Allie Joubert, for he knew about her, but over what had been said just before that, asked, "Going into the ravine? Who?"

Dillon turned his large, doggish face towards him.

"I regret that I wasn't able to be more frank," he said. Meares thought he did not look particularly regretful. "It was a question of risk, you understand. The fewer people who know these things, the less risk."

"Risk? What risk? To who?" Meares was now finding difficulty in avoiding outright tetchiness, beginning to suspect that in spite of his unreserved co-operation with these men, he might still have been misled in some way.

"To one of our men," said Dillon urbanely. "One of Mr Culley's own close colleagues, in point of fact."

"I reckon you'd best start from the beginning," Meares said. This, it seemed was what you got for readily making South-Western facilities available to people from the Treasury. A lack of frankness. Apparently Culley read the mention of his own name as a cue to come into the discussion.

"First, we have to work on the belief that all those others who went up into that ravine missed something," he said, and when Meares, removing the cheroot from his teeth, looked set to interrupt, went on quickly, "We have to be quite certain about that ravine before we can even start thinking about where else Chandler might have hidden those sacks. So we've sent one of our men in there to take one more

53

good look, take his time and work his way from the bottom to the top of that place. He's a good man. His name's Vern Ulrich, and he'll look like any other fossicker, pack-horse and implements and all. And in any case, if I do get other information we'll likely need another man on hand."

"Then damn' good luck to him," said Meares feelingly, "for God knows our own people did all that and didn't come out with so much as a dirty dollar-bill." Clearly he thought that not only were they about to waste more of their time, but were also, in a sense, demeaning the efforts of all those who had tried before, especially those from the South-Western railroad, and failed.

"And there is, of course," said Culley, choosing not to react in any way to Meares's choler, "this line of enquiry of mine right here in Gaspard. It could well turn up the answer."

Well, they *had* told Meares about that. Unthinkingly, though, he said what Dillon had said already. "You mean Mrs Joubert?"

"Yes. But of course that's by no means a matter that can be rushed."

Meares thought it was possible to read that in a number of different ways, but he said, "Assuming, of course, that there's anything to find out."

Dillon said smoothly, "We've not been entirely asleep, Mr Meares. We do find that where people are concerned, where large amounts of money are involved, then sooner or later the whispers begin. Oh, not for quite some time, perhaps, but eventually. Eventually."

"This Mrs Joubert, you've said all along that she did know Chandler."

"Not necessarily *know*, but it's quite possible. What we do know is she went several times to the Warbeck jail while he was being held there. It's true she went with a preacher, but it does seem, now, that at other times she went alone; and then, after Chandler had been shot, Mrs Joubert was on hand too, helping to minister to him. Er, yes, I expect that's the word."

To Meares, chewing on his cheroot now, it sounded like a quite tenuous link, but then, after all, it was not a waste of S-W's time and money that was involved here but the Treasury's, so he kept his mouth shut.

As though following Meares's doubting thoughts, Culley went on, "I've got a strong feeling I might be getting closer to finding out what it is Al . . . what Mrs Joubert knows, if she knows *anything*. It could be quite soon, sooner than I'd thought earlier."

Pillow-talk, probably, thought Meares, and when that notion came to him, so too did his recollection of the woman he had seen walking with Culley, and he savoured that, and even felt a slight arousal. There was something compelling, something *sensuous* about her, the way she looked and moved. When next he glanced at Culley it was to see the grey-suited man smiling faintly at him and staring at him unwinkingly.

* * *

Allie Joubert was in her spartan little room at May Callan's rooming-house, a clean, quiet place, conservative and unremarkable; and comparatively inexpensive. It was, Allie thought, a reassuringly anonymous place to stay during the time she was in Gaspard. True, May Callan, more liberal in other ways, still insisted that all callers wait in the lobby, and it was there that Stace Culley had taken to making appearances from time to time, to go strolling out with Allie; by no means every evening though, for his work at the Red Deuce allowed him limited time to himself after sundown. But through some arrangement he had come to with Toop, who owned the Deuce, he did stop by occasionally at night. Sometimes they would walk to the small house which apparently

Culley had rented near the southern edge of the town.

Culley. She had thought about him a great deal since she had come to know him, an attractive man, courteous, displaying almost what she thought of as Southern manners as far as women were concerned, with an appealing way of expressing himself that was an echo from a world she had thought to have vanished.

So in recent weeks she had been much engaged by considerations of whether or not she could trust him unreservedly. Some time soon she was going to have to work out a detailed plan to get to the place where the money was. Tomorrow she must make it her business to buy a riding-skirt, and thereafter, be seen taking exercise, with Stace Culley at her side, riding out and about with a certain regularity so that people would become accustomed to seeing her coming and going, and after a little while take no particular notice.

Culley. Perhaps, though he was taller and dressed in much finer clothes, she was attracted to him because he reminded her in some ways of Stagg, his finely-planed face, his thin moustache, his air of near-gentility. Poor old Staggie. Well, with care and a certain degree of luck she would soon recompense herself for the loss of Stagg and all the plans they had made; and although she still felt an odd hesitation about it, if it meant that to achieve her purpose she must take Stace Culley into her confidence, then so be it.

★ ★ ★

Of several similar establishments in Gaspard, the Gaspard House Hotel was by far the best appointed, and as far as business transactions were concerned the place to take the clients was the long, richly-panelled dining-room there. This was a place of subdued conversations and mutedly-clicking cutlery and the unhurried, assured movements of livened waiters and neat and decorous waitresses.

It was over this impressive room that Marion Gowan presided with a calm competence, attending to reservations, resolving problems, remembering who was who, with what was almost a gentle brand of flattery. Known to be the estranged wife of the Slane County sheriff, since she had come to Gaspard and to the hotel there were those among the Gaspard matrons, observing her small, slim roundness, her fair skin and her hair the colour of ripe corn and very dark blue eyes, who were, of course, more than a little wary of her. Plenty of their menfolk liked to dine at the Gaspard House.

Malpass was one who did. And Hetty Malpass, a round doll of a woman with a too-large mouth, invariably came with him, firmly attached to his arm. They had been in there this evening along with two lumber-buyers, large men with rough hands, raw men who looked as though they had been crammed into their town suits by main force.

Marion Gowan was well aware that Malpass watched her, and whenever he could, tried to catch her eye in one of the large, ornate wall-mirrors. Vaguely Marion wondered how the woman who worked in his lumber-yard office, Allie Joubert, handled Arne Malpass.

Now, after the evening's busiest time had come and gone, Marion, seated at her partitioned-off desk near the main doors, reflected again on Allie Joubert. Marion had not met her in Warbeck, knowing her only by sight, but she did realize that over recent weeks there had arisen one or two strong rumours about her, and whether or not she really did know something about the robbery of the South-Western freight. Well, perhaps she did, perhaps not.

Marion sighed. That would be Allie Joubert's problem. Marion had problems of her own. From the pocket of her neat black skirt she again took the letter that had come several days ago from her husband, Bob Gowan. What he was suggesting was that they must talk. They must set past problems aside and sit down quietly and discuss the future; decide, in effect, if indeed they still *had* a future. He could not accept, he said, that the present situation meant the end of their life together. He was prepared to admit freely that there were faults which were his, and he would not seek to excuse them. He merely wished to talk.

She put the repeatedly-read letter away. She had not answered it, knowing that he would likely read that as acquiescence, for his letter had had a sense of urgency about it; so she believed he would come, but to what outcome she could not even begin to predict.

Idly she wondered what Gowan's views were now, on Allie Joubert. Gowan had taken some appalling risks in the shooting at Warbeck, had never shrunk from what he saw as his duty; and that had been a large part of their own problem.

But as far as the Joubert woman had been concerned, Gowan had made no move to detain her or to follow her. Maybe if he did come to Gaspard and set eyes on her again he might take a fresh view; or he might take good care not to become involved, because this was not his territory, yet mainly for fear of alienating Marion herself before they had a chance to try to resolve their own problems.

Truly she did not know what she would say or do if Gowan did come. At the present time she was basking in her independence, yet for a reason she could not even begin to fathom, she had begun to have a feeling of foreboding and it had come over her with the arrival of Gowan's letter.

* * *

One of the Gaspard deputies, Rafe Collis, having been up to the Red Deuce ostensibly to run his eye over the crowd there but, as Macken

63

knew, almost certainly to have a flutter himself, now came back into the county office where Macken was still working at papers.

Macken glanced up, sensing that there was something else on Collis's mind.

"What's up?"

"Not sure," Collis said and took off his hat and half threw it onto a wooden peg on the wall. "Some new faces around. Old-fashioned faces."

"Up at the Deuce?"

"No, up around Caine's livery. Bunch o' hard boys with a pack-animal along. All sweat an' dust an' no shit taken; but one thing I did hear was that one of 'em could be that Rad Nash."

Macken had picked up another paper but now put it down. "Now, that's a name I've heard, an' all the tales have been bad ones. Yeah. His brother was one o' them pricks that Gowan blew away in Warbeck."

"So I heard," Collis said. "Want me

to go take another look, ask around?"

Macken shook his head slowly. "Let it go fer now. We'll keep an eye out. Tell the other boys when yuh can. Look an' listen. But they might jes' be here to sink a few to lay the dust, hit the whorehouse an' move on." Macken looked as though he did not truly believe it himself.

5

STARTLED, seeing the line of diluted grey down the side of the window-shade, Allie sat up; then the flowing creaminess of her body could just be discerned as she slipped quickly from the bed and began gathering up her clothes.

Among the rumpled covers behind her — in his own bed — Stace Culley began stirring now, and soon became aware that the weight of the other person was no longer beside him, and next he reached out for matches to light a bedside lamp.

"No . . . " Allie's soft voice was pitched low but her tone was urgent. "No lights. I've got to go, Stace, right now, and go quietly. I don't want to be seen leaving here at this hour."

Culley was struggling to free himself of tangled bedclothes.

"I'm real sorry, Allie." He stepped out onto the cold floor, picked up his pocket-watch from the bedside table, and naked, crossed to the shaded window, there in marginally better light to peer at the numerals. "Christ. Wait, I'll dress and come with you, see you safe to Mrs Callan's."

She shook her head to dissuade him. "No, better not. I'll be all right, Stace. Truly. After all it's not so far." She was dressing hurriedly, feeling thankful now that, earlier — last night — she had not loosened and let fall her long hair as he had persistently wanted her to, for now there would have been precious time wasted in putting it up again. Not that she had intended staying with him as long as this, but they had both drifted into a gentle love-sleep.

He was still far from happy about it.

"I should come with you."

"No."

"You'll be walking on back-streets, and even at this hour there could be men wandering around. You have to be on your guard in this town, Allie. And some real rough boys have come in lately. Drifters. And a man named Nash is here with some other hard-noses. People are walking wide around them, and from what I hear with good reason."

She was smoothing her dark-blue dress down over her hips and made herself carry on doing it without even glancing at him, as though quite preoccupied.

"Who?"

"Some man called Rad Nash. They do say that he's kin to one of the men who tried to break Jack Chandler out of the Warbeck jail that time. You'd know about that, anyway."

"Oh yes." Then, "I was right there in Warbeck when all of that happened. I told you, didn't I? I didn't get to see much of what went on, on that particular day, but I do remember the name Nash being talked about as one of the men who'd been killed." She did look at him then, but in this grey gloom he was unable to read the expression on her face. "And then, eventually, we did what we could for that man Chandler, after he'd got out of the jail and been shot."

"Shot by a lawman named Gowan, so I heard," said Culley. "Shot in the back."

"Yes, shot in the back. Twice. They carried Chandler into the saloon where it had happened. He'd gone right out through a window onto the street. The saloon, that's where he died, laid out on tables they'd pushed together. I went in there along with a friend of mine, a Warbeck preacher, Mr Crowder, but there was nothing at all that either of us could do." It was all said in a matter-of-fact way. Now she was ready to leave and she said again, "I'll be all right. Don't go worrying about me, Stace."

There were questions tumbling around in his head that he still wanted to ask her but he knew that this was not the time, so he made no further objection as she brushed a warm kiss across his lips and left quietly.

Most of the previous afternoon they had spent riding hired horses, heading out of Gaspard in a southerly direction, in no particular hurry, and Allie had said she had been glad to get away from the town for an hour or two. When at last they had returned to the livery corral she had made her way back to her room at Callan's, while Culley had gone home to change before heading off to his work at the Red Deuce. Later in the evening, though, she had met him and that was when she had gone with him directly to his house, a small but well-kept place which, had anyone given the matter any investigation, would have been discovered to be the property of the South-Western railroad.

Now Culley set about heating water for a bath, and as he went about this mundane task, pondered over these past few hours and marvelled at the marked advance in his relationship with

Allie Joubert. Lovers now. With a jolt of surprise, Culley found that he was being pulled two ways, one of which was undeniably agreeable, the other unpleasant, for he had found this woman compellingly attractive; more so, indeed, than any other woman he had ever known — and in his time he had known plenty — and yet his vowed purpose here was to deceive her. If she did know anything at all about the money from the train, then he must make it his unswerving business to find out exactly what it was; but he knew that to get as far as that he would need to step very carefully. It had not taken him long to discover that Allie was by no means a fool, and if she *had* got information directly from Chandler, then when, a short time ago, she had talked openly of the man and his dying on tables in a Warbeck saloon, she had done so with superb calm, her low-pitched voice betraying not the slighest disquiet, telling him frankly that she had not only been there on the night

71

Jack Chandler died but, with others, had tried to ease his last minutes. No pretence. No hesitations. Well at least he could take some satisfaction, he supposed, that the Chandler matter had been broached between them and he could now follow it up. But with great care.

In her room at May Callan's Allie was much relieved to be there, having come unseen she believed through the always-open lobby, and having come with slow, shoeless steps up the narrow stairs to her room.

Once inside, she sat down on the edge of the iron-framed bed, then swung her legs up and lay back with her head and shoulders against the pillows. She was thinking about Stace Culley. What had begun as just another pleasant interlude had gone in an easy and natural way much, much further than she had ever intended at the outset, but she was still oddly unsure what her true feelings were about Culley.

It was certain that from the first she had been strongly drawn to him, yet in spite of all that had developed between them there was still *something* that was giving her pause, sounding some inexplicable warning. It was not what he was, how he chose to earn his living; it was not that, so far, he had volunteered almost nothing about his origins, much less about his more recent past. And the man himself, the physical Culley, was almost too good-looking, too much like Staggie, perhaps, but more polished in speech and manner than him. There was a greater depth to Culley and she felt there were things that were being held back. Ruefully, as these very thoughts came to her, she had to admit, almost with self-contempt, that her own reticence with Culley was even less agreeable, founded as it was upon secrecy and deception. *Allie Joubert. Stagg's woman.* Yet how had they got onto the dangerous subject of Jack Chandler and Warbeck and all that business there? Nash, that was how. Culley had spoken about this Rad Nash being here. She did not know the man, however, and indeed she had not known the other Nash either, the one who had been shot to death in Warbeck. That one had clearly been a man whom the Chandler brothers or maybe Pearce had known from some earlier time and who had been somehow persuaded to take part in the attempt to break Jack Chandler out of the county jail, no doubt for a generous share of the spoils. But when, at Culley's, the name had suddenly come up it had shocked her, and the once-actress had had to draw upon all her hard-learned skills to conceal from Culley any visible reaction.

Allie felt a fresh stirring of unease. It was similar to the one she had experienced when, in the euphoric wake of intimacy, having stepped almost to the brink of confiding everything to Stace Culley, suddenly and for unaccountable reasons she had drawn back. Even warm and hard-breathing against the body of her lover she had decided that, for the moment at least, she would simply go on as she had been doing, stay close to Culley certainly, go out riding with him, get the curious tongue-waggers accustomed to seeing her taking regular exercise, and bide her time. She could afford to wait just a little while longer before deciding.

In recent days information had fallen into her hands that had relieved her mind immeasurably and it had come about as an unexpected bonus and, oddly, because of the fact that she was employed by Malpass.

In a dingy storeroom next to the yard office, looking for other papers, she had come upon a number of maps of the Fayette Hills region, the timber-slopes and the area leading up to the mountains, the High Torres, rough terrain, riven with ancient canyons and split with difficult ravines, a place of bluffs and crags and slab-rock, dry and unappealing; and in one part was clearly shown the secret place, the much sought-after place where Jack Chandler had gone in and hidden the money plundered from the South-Western. She had known the name of it and a particular feature of it, for Chandler himself had told it to her. Now she knew the exact location and how to get to it, and once there, what to look for. The final piece had dropped into place without her having to make any enquiries at all that might have aroused suspicion.

* * *

Marion Gowan, in her room at the Gaspard House, lay wakeful in the early morning, and as soon as she had opened her eyes she had thought of her husband, Bob Gowan.

He was coming to Gaspard. A telegram had now confirmed it. She had experienced a most curious feeling about that, a sense of pleasurable anticipation and yet a sense of dread. Separated from him for long enough to want to see him again, she was now apprehensive of what might so easily turn out to be an abrasive meeting, a confrontation in which might surface forcefully, brutally, for the first time, their mutual disgreements, a sorry and bitter spectacle of blame and counter-blame. If it did, she did not know if she would be able to endure it.

But in the past they had gone on too long using charged silences as a means of rebuke. When at last the words did begin to flow, she thought, they might well come in such a dam-burst of acrimony that they raised fresh walls of resentment which might endure well into the future, walls perhaps never to be broken down.

Other matters had become of concern to her and she did not know whether she was pleased or flattered or ashamed about them. Men, some of them not unattractive, had begun making it plain to her that she was viewed in Gaspard as a desirable woman. So far she had managed to keep her distance, to disengage herself discreetly from too-close contact, to withdraw gently, taking care, though, never to give outright offence.

Her history was known, of that she was quite sure, not through her own discussion of it but by the inevitable gossip that would have followed her here, a woman alone, seeking work, preferring her own company, unwilling to be drawn into intimacy with either men or women. An estranged wife. And now Gowan was coming and that would draw eyes and ears, promote fresh speculation, yet it was not wholly that which had begun to concern Marion. It was the apprehension — no, more, the fear — that because of who Gowan was and what he was, some kind of violence would come here with him.

6

THE elongated, brick-built and multi-windowed building known as the East Hotel, was in truth a whorehouse.

On the night that Allie Joubert had gone with Culley to his house and to his bed, Nash, Brophy, Staples and Bascom, having issued somewhat unsteadily and certainly very rowdily from Leary's dirty Lucky Spin saloon, immediately hit the East, Brophy in the lead and unbuckling his thick shell-belt while still going through the lobby.

The first problem occurred when Maggie Otis, plump and baggy in her shapeless house-coat, the woman whose lucrative enterprise this was, came out of what she called her office, saying that it was a busy night and they would all have to wait their turn.

Brophy, now holding shell-belt, holster

and heavy pistol, told her that waiting around downstairs for whores was not one of the things that he did willingly, and therefore started up the boot-scraped stairs, the man with the rope-scarred neck, Staples, and the flat-nosed Bascom following him, laughing, Nash strolling to the stairs in their wake.

Maggie Otis did not argue with them but instead started shouting, "Ez! Ez, you're wanted!"

"Ez must be the goddamn yard-dawg," Bascom said, pausing on the stairs.

"He ain't," said Maggie, and this soon proved to be the case.

Out of a narrow, lightless passage that passed to one side of the stairway there appeared a very big, muscular man wearing black cord pants and a filthy, pinkish wool undervest, a man carrying a sawn-off 10-gauge with a brass frame.

Summing up this new situation at once Nash called, "Wait!" and those who were already on the stairs stopped and looked back, at first not perceiving the reason; then the big man, Ezzard, came slowly into view, the drab lamplight of the lobby glancing from the short, ugly barrel of the shotgun.

They were hard men, all of them, but Ezzard had come to a stop only three feet away from Nash. A sawn-off at that range would be ignored only by the congenitally stupid. Nerve had nothing whatsoever to do with it.

For such a large, muscular man, Ezzard had a curiously high-pitched voice, something which in any other circumstances Brophy for one would have loudly held up to ridicule; but there was no hint of derision when Ezzard said, "Boys, yuh heard what Maggie said. Nobody goes up 'til she gives the word."

Very slowly Nash turned but kept his right hand well clear of the butt of his pistol. "Which means," said Ezzard, "yuh kin wait down here or yuh kin leave."

Those on the stairs were affronted but uncertain and there were not even the smallest moves made, for Ezzard was immovably there like some ponderous, dangerous bear, his foreshortened shotgun pointing motionlessly at Nash.

Maggie Otis now came closer. "That's a whole lot better, boys. Now look, you're real welcome here but there's other boys up there right now, so why don't you sit around awhile, through here (one of her pudgy hands gesturing towards a doorway behind her) an' I'll go fetch us a bottle to pass the time?"

Those on the stairs came down slowly, but Brophy said, "We already had all the coffin-varnish we want, fer now."

Nash looked at him briefly, then said to Maggie, "Why, we take that offer real kindly, ma-am, but if it's all the same we'll leave now an' we'll come back later. We sure do apologize fer bustin' in this way. It warn't seemly." Nash spoke easily, quietly, the very soul of reason, and even Maggie Otis was somewhat taken aback. Certainly those who were with Nash were visibly surprised but they all kept their traps shut and followed him outside.

Inside, Maggie said to Ezzard, "That's a relief. I thought for sure that bunch was gonna cut up real ugly. They looked bad enough to burn."

Ezzard licked his thick lips and then, because he was a man who took precautions, and moving lightly for such a big man, went across the lobby to the street door and looked out, both ways; but he was back in again just as soon.

"They've sure gone, Mrs Otis. No sign." Indeed, the very night seemed to have swallowed them.

Macken had hung around the office for longer than usual but had departed now leaving Bob Sloane and Artie Reece to see out the evening hours. Sloane had not long come in again from a stroll along Main and his report was brief.

"Dead as Boot Hill."

Leaving, Macken asked, "No sight o' that crowd Rafe was talkin' about?"

"Nothin' I seen," said Reece, "but I did hear tell they're still around Gaspard. They was in the Deuce, an' went on to Leary's."

Macken, rawboned, baggy-eyed, a man seemingly beyond either surprise or undue expectation, nodded and departed. But he had had an odd feeling in his gut over recent hours, nothing physical, more of a strange sense of unreality, foreboding even, of unpleasant events pending. He wondered if Collis had gone home — which happened to be Alderney's Rooming-house — or more likely had headed for the Red Deuce for a quick turn of the cards. As a deputy, Macken could find no major fault with Collis, but he still held some unspoken reservations about a young man who seemed to have become drawn to the gambling habit. As this particular thought came to him again now, Macken, crossing over Main, silently castigated himself. *Puritanical bastard.*

His own three-room house provided by the county as an adjunct to the office and in which he now lived alone, stood on one of Gaspard's unsalubrious back-streets, and he was headed in that direction now. It was a quiet night.

By this time Hank Ezzard had unloaded his sawn-off 10-gauge and stored it away in a closet under the stairs and he went now into the big, cluttered kitchen, there to pour himself a mug of coffee and feeling more than satisfied with the outcome of recent events. First, however, he crossed to the windows to draw the shades and that was when his ear caught the sound of someone calling in a hushed yet urgent way: "Ez? Ez?" Ezzard cupped one of his large hands to the dark, reflective, smeared glass, doing his best to peer out into the yard, but he could see no movement there. It was nothing alarming. Sometimes panhandlers came, regarding Maggie Otis's yard door as the place for a soft touch. Ezzard crossed and drew the bolts and opened the door.

The black eye of Brophy's .44 pistol was almost touching Ezzard's left eye.

"So here we are ag'in," said Brophy.

Slowly but without hesitation Hank Ezzard began retreating, Brophy, the arm holding the long pistol almost fully extended, following him inside; then came Staples and Bascom and then Nash, who closed the door behind him.

"Where's that chopped-off pipe?" Nash asked.

Ezzard knew very well that to hesitate in answering would be to bring instantly a reaction of a kind which he would not wish even to contemplate, so he led them to the stair-closet where the 10-gauge was.

"In there."

In the pallid light issuing from the lobby, Nash stepped closer and opened the closet, peered inside, felt around then said, "Ah," and took the 10-gauge out.

Before Ezzard had time to realize what was happening, his arms were seized and pinioned by Bascom and Staples, while Brophy, stepping aside and lowering the pistol, allowed Nash enough elbow-room to come in close, holding the stubby shotgun, and drive the single barrel savagely into Ezzard's solar plexus.

What erupted from the big man's mouth was something between a shout and a scream, and when his head jerked down with the jack-knifing of his body, even with his arms held, Nash whipped the heavy stock of the gun up in a powerful arc to strike Ezzard across the mouth and nose to punch his head upwards again, bright blood springing from him. Ezzard, released by Bascom and Staples, sat down so heavily that the very floor seemed to shake.

Nash broke open the 10-gauge, and holding it by the stumpy barrel, began bashing the thick stock against a newel-post, so it was a toss-up whether gun-stock or post would break first. In the event it was the stock of the shotgun, and Nash went on swinging until it was all but smashed off, then dropped what remained of the weapon to the floor.

Maggie Otis soon arrived of course, but taking it all in at a glance, had enough old-fashioned wit to keep her distance and not open her mouth.

"No bastard in some fly-blown, clap-struck, stinkin' whorehouse ever points one o' them things at me an' walks away," Nash said, "an' if you (stabbing a finger at Maggie) if you got hold o' some notion o' sendin' fer some fartin' badge-carrier, then yuh ain't got the brains yuh climbed out o' your cot with."

Without a further word to her or even another glance, Nash, Bascom, Staples and Brophy went trooping upstairs and after a very short interval there came the sounds of flimsy doors being flung open and men shouting and women screaming.

Maggie Otis could only stand watching sadly as several of her regulars began coming down the stairs in various states of undress, one in fact stark-naked and carrying shirt, boots and pants, hopping to get a leg into the pants only after he arrived in the lobby.

"Whoever them bastards are," muttered Maggie, though not to anyone in particular, "I sure do hope they ain't come to this town permanent."

In another part of the town a lone horseman drew to a halt outside a seedy building in a street off Main, a structure with a lantern burning in the porch, illuminating a sign which said HOTEL.

The rider, a tall, angular man, slightly stooped, sat for a moment or two rubbing slowly at stubble on his jaw, trying to decide whether to get down and go inside or walk the horse up and down a few more streets seeking a more agreeable-looking place to stay.

Already aware that there were bigger, more pleasant hotels in Gaspard, he did not have a lot of money at his disposal and could see no point in wasting what he did have on fancy lodgings. It was true that he had brought with him a small roll of extra bills but these were intended for a distinctly different purpose.

Bob Gowan expelled a long, tired breath from ballooned cheeks and swung stiffly down out of the saddle. He undid the studs of his thick jacket and hitched at the heavily-shelled belt and holstered Smith and Wesson Schofield around his middle, then still moving stiffly, walked his horse forward and tied it to the warped rail of the porch.

Faint light was showing from some of the shaded windows and when he opened the door he saw that there was a pale amber-shaded lamp in the lobby. The place smelled of mould and of fried food and he guessed that it looked and smelled a hell of a lot different from where his wife, Marion, was at this particular moment.

Marion, in a comfortable, clean bed in a small but well-furnished room at the Gaspard House, though it had been a busy, tiring evening, was still wakeful, wondering when Gowan might elect to show up, and wondering too, what she could possibly say to him when he did come. Sometimes it did seem to her that their parting had been too definite, too brutal almost, for either of them to entertain any thoughts of a reconciliation; and it had been her move, in the end, not Gowan's, and she had simply got on the train to Gaspard while he had been not only away from the house, but still weathering the aftermath of a fierce gun-battle.

But in truth they had lost contact long before she had made up her mind to move away from Warbeck, as though in some odd manner they had both abandoned the will or did not have the capacity to find appropriate words, so that, over time, a veritable desert of silence had formed between them. Yet there had been frequent occasions since she had come here to Gaspard that Marion had known feelings of real uncertainty, and yes, if she were to admit it, guilt. Not only had it been she who had ultimately made the break, but she had chosen to do it when Gowan himself had gone through a time of acute danger and was trying to hold a whole lot of things together.

Gowan, too, at that time, had been monstrously deceived by his own deputy, Augie Telfer, though Gowan had finally caught and killed the terrible Jack Chandler during a night of frightening violence. Marion wondered not only what Gowan, but others in Warbeck, had thought about what would have been seen as her desertion at a time when she must have known that at any tick of the clock, in carrying out his duty, he might have been badly hit and disabled or even shot to death. So there was that awful burden for her to carry as well; and in no way could that be separated from the other problems that there had been between them. Defensively, but without much hope, she thought, *"But maybe he won't come, after all."*

The noise which had erupted inside the East Hotel had to some extent abated. Nash and the others were still in there, but now all in the room where Brophy lay naked his animal smell prevailing even over the cloying perfume of the coffee-coloured whore, Estelle, who still lay with him among the rumpled, tainted bedclothes in an iron four-poster.

"It's long past time we talked," Nash said. "Time we got our heads right about this goddamn' train money. I got a few more notions about it. What I reckon is, we've shit round in that ravine long enough." Nash, as time had gone on, had begun to thread together one or two vagrant whispers that had been blowing around for quite a while, some that he had not taken too seriously at first, in fact not until fatigue and repeated failure had overtaken him, and was now driving Nash to cast about for other possibilities. His overriding belief now was that there had to be a better approach.

Bascom of the flat nose glanced at the naked, sweat-filmed whore. "What about her?"

"Don't worry about this one," Brophy said and reached with one hand and tapped her on her full lips. She drew back, but grinning, made quick, graceful movements with her delicate fingers. Brophy laughed, pushed at her, turning her half over, and slapped at a sleek buttock. "She don't hear an she don't talk, this li'l dove." He, too, was grinning widely. "But otherwise, Estelle, she's dynamite."

"Yeah, yeah," said Nash.

"What's on your mind?" Staples asked. Today the scar on his neck seemed more livid than ever.

"There's been some word that's got around," Nash said, "that ought to be looked into."

"Such as?" asked Brophy.

"Such as the woman that knowed a feller called Stagg, who was at that train, mebbe knows somethin' else."

"Stagg. Him that got his lamp blowed out?" asked Bascom. "Him that was in with the Chandlers fer years?"

"Yeah," said Nash. "Well, this woman, her name's Allie Joubert an' she's in this town, so I hear."

"So, Stagg dead at the train, where was she?"

"In Warbeck, or headin' fer Warbeck. An' she was right on hand when Chandler cashed in."

"So yuh reckon she knows somethin'?"

Nash shrugged. "Some says it's so. It ain't much, but we ain't got nothin' else. From Warbeck, she only come as far as this. Yuh got to wonder why."

They would all tend to grasp at anything now, having spent so many fruitless days in that fly-ridden, stifling ravine.

"Where's this Joubert woman at?"

"I dunno," said Nash, "but I'll sure find out in jig-time."

"Then what?"

"We'll decide then what as it comes," said Nash, "but we won't go shittin' all over the chance, if there is one, by shoutin' it to every other bastard in Gaspard. Leave this Allie Joubert to me."

7

THE thin, somewhat sad-looking deputy, Artie Reece, leaning against the door-frame, knew when he was being lied to, but there were frequent scuffles at the East Hotel and its environs, so Reece was not about to get himself too wound up about it. It was simply that, in passing, he had noticed that Hank Ezzard seemed to have been violently worked over, and that was unusual.

"Musta been a real big customer," observed Reece, "to git all that done to yuh, Hank. I ain't gonna find a corpse lyin' round somewhere, am I? If that should be the case, Macken, he'd be sure to catch fire, the mood he's been in lately."

Ezzard's ham-like, ravaged face, his naturally thick lips cut and further puffed up, and behind that mess the probability of broken teeth, looked hurt and sullen. A lesser man, thought Reece, would not be on his feet at all. Ezzard gave a brief shake of the head. "Been an' gone," he said, the words barely comprehensible.

"Local?" Reece was yawning, however, when he asked the question, so it could reasonably be assumed that he did not much care one way or the other. When Ezzard, abandoning further utterance, simply shrugged, Reece said, "It's jes' that I did find out that some real hard boys are in town." The shifty look that Ezzard gave him before the injured man's glance slid away said it plainly enough for Reece but he could not resist saying, "Thought yuh had a sawn-off to help yuh git the hard points made, Hank."

Maggie Otis, coming in, hearing some of what Reece had said, eyed the lounging deputy without enthusiasm, but warily. Artie Reece was a man whose mood could shift disconcertingly; yet she could not resist asking:

98

"Yuh come here for a girl, or what, Artie?"

"Me? Naw, can't afford the prices," Reece said, "an' anyway, sooner or later Etta would git to hear of it an' burn yuh out. Etta ain't as good-tempered as me."

"Line o' duty's been known to stretch some in my place for more'n one o' your callin'," Maggie said, stone-faced but not about to push it too far in case Reece did one of his celebrated turnarounds.

Reece, however, smiling bleakly, knew that in all likelihood Maggie was getting at Rafe Collis, but having had enough for the present of the East Hotel, he shoved away from his leaning posture and departed, his boots scuffing across the yard.

Elsewhere, Nash had just concluded the sale, to a small, fat, greasy man named Spurle, of a sturdy, good-quality saddler, no brand, no questions.

And elsewhere at about this time, Marion Gowan, having come outside the Gaspard House Hotel, a light green-coloured cape slipped over her trim shoulders, was now about to depart, saying that while it was nice to see him, right now did not happen to be a good time. If they were to talk properly it would have to be later.

Gowan, even more gaunt than she had ever seen him, but clean-shaven and alert, nodded his understanding. If he was disconcerted he was taking very good care not to show it.

"I plan on being here for a few days," Gowan told her. *As long as it takes* was what he did not say. If, in the past, she had always had the power to stir him, she did so now to no less a degree, with her small-framed trimness, only a bit over five feet of her, with her hair the colour of ripe corn, gold-threaded, and her large, very dark blue eyes. Ten years younger than Gowan, she looked as though the difference must be nearer to twenty, and she moved like it too, with an unconscious light grace, the carriage of a girl.

Gowan was indeed disappointed, having hoped to talk with her now and at length and had prepared himself for it as best he could, but he was smart enough not to rush the matter now, for as he saw it, he had at least achieved the first of what he hoped would be a series of positive steps, he had made contact with her after a lengthy interval and she had not seemed displeased to see him. Well, to be honest, neither pleased nor displeased. Reserved and very calm. In control.

She started to turn away, then paused. "Will? How is Will?"

"Improving," said Gowan, "slowly." Will Hutchison, now the regular deputy in Warbeck, replacing the dead Augie Telfer, was lucky to be still alive, hit hard as he had been in one arm by Pearce's .45 carbine, a wound that Doc Groves had not liked the looks of at all and that Hutchison himself had more than once been convinced was turning gangrenous. Since being wounded Hutchison had been moving quite slowly, an unsettling reminder for all who saw him of the break-out of Jack Chandler and the sudden deaths at Warbeck.

"I'm pleased. He's a good man, Bob, and he didn't deserve that."

Again Gowan nodded. This time she did turn away and vanished into the dim interior of the Gaspard House. *Later* she had said to him.

Suddenly left at a loose end Gowan looked up and down the long main street at all the activity there, all of which, as a mere visitor, was of no interest to him. The only person in this busy place that he wished to see and to talk with had just walked away and left him standing. So he too now wandered away along the boardwalk, looking up to where the office of the Delmar county jail stood. Ed Macken. He might just as well drift along and pass a word or two with Ed, fill in some time.

Macken, hard, stringy and sun-dried, a man of Gowan's age, or more, rose to grip his hand.

"Heard yuh'd come in, Bob. Word about it got around real quick. You're a man o' some account hereabouts, what with the Chandlers an' all that crowd an' the hullabaloo in Warbeck."

"A reputation unasked an' undeserved," Gowan said. "It solved nothing. For one thing, we never did find any of the money they got away with, an' when you come to sum it all up, Ed, the law hunted Jack down an' took him to Warbeck an' in the finish it was the law that let him out."

"Well, whatever it was drove Augie Telfer to that, he sure paid for it," Macken observed.

"Oh, he did that," agreed Gowan.

Macken knew the man opposite well enough to be able to say, also, "I knew that Marion come here, Bob, an' in fact I've passed a word with her from time to time. No questions, only a passin' word."

"She's the one an' only reason I'm here," Gowan said. "Over the next day or two we have to find time to talk, me an' Marion."

How much of the detail Macken actually knew was by no means clear for he did not pursue that matter, merely looking frankly at Gowan and nodding, but he did say then, "About the same time Marion got into Gaspard, that other woman from Warbeck did too. Allie Joubert."

Gowan's leather-faced expression was unreadable, but he asked, "What do you make of Mrs Joubert, Ed?"

"I've not seen fit to talk with her at all," Macken said. "I've had no firm reason to; but I've seen her around Gaspard. She works for Arne Malpass in his lumber-yard office. An' it's clear she's tight with a feller called Stace Culley that deals faro up at the Red Deuce. Somethin' of a Fancy Dan, is Culley. I ain't made my mind up about that feller neither." Macken's eyes pinned Gowan's. "There's been opinions on the breeze, Bob, about this Mrs Joubert."

Gowan, his large hands clasped behind him, took a pace or two up the dusty room, turned, came back and stopped, looking speculatively at Macken. "It happens I heard a few tales as well," he said, "after she'd gone. If there was anything to any of it, she was real fly about the matter, an' if there *was* I'm going to wind up looking somewhat of a fool in Warbeck, for she was there, right enough, under my nose while it was all going on."

Macken thought he might as well stop pussyfooting and ask right out. "Bob, *could* she have found out anything from Jack Chandler?"

"Oh, yeah, thinking back, it was sure possible. Yeah, she was along at the jail a time or two with a sing-song preacher we got up there, Crowder. They came offering the good word, an' comfort. Came on her own, sometimes, as well; an' it's true she was in Kelly's saloon that night — came with Crowder — when Jack Chandler expired. She was there all through, working round him, sponging his head an' such, an' he wasn't out to it the whole time. Yeah, looking back, there were plenty of chances." He smiled, but humourlessly. "Always took Crowder for a fool. Maybe the bigger fool was me."

"After a goddamn' shoot like that one? You're bein' a mite hard on yourself, Bob."

"No," Gowan said, "not near hard enough." And Macken, staring soberly at him, was unable to make up his mind whether or not Gowan was still talking only about the Warbeck shoot. Then Gowan said, "This man Culley, tell me about him."

Macken pursed his lips. "Come to Gaspard on'y a matter of a month or two back, from where I don't know. Like I said, he deals faro, an' he runs a few other games there. By all accounts he's a sharp performer." Gowan thought that Macken looked almost sheepish when he added, "One o' my deputies here, Rafe Collis, is somewhat inclined by nature towards games o' chance an' he's got to know this Culley some, but from what Collis says, Culley ain't a man to give out much about hisself."

"And you say Culley's tight with Allie Joubert?"

"Yea. Seen 'em walkin' around Gaspard together. Calls on her too. Takes her out ridin' an' all. Got to admit she's a real han'some woman, Mrs Joubert. Heads off Culley by a year or two though, I'd say." He looked shrewdly at Gowan. "It got to yuh, did it, Bob, not gettin' even a whiff o' that train-money o' Jack's?"

"It did that," said Gowan frankly, "but it wasn't only that, or the amount of it, or who it belonged to. There'd been too many left lying dead over it, an' not only in Warbeck but out there at that train. It was a slaughterhouse, Ed. Those men didn't deserve that."

Macken wiped a large, rawboned hand around his face in a rather weary gesture, looked down then up again at

Gowan as though coming to a decision after having given the matter all due consideration, and he said, "When they all come in an' tried to git Jack out o' that cage o' yours there was a man called Nash among 'em, or so I heard."

"There was," Gowan said. "We shot him off his horse when they were out on the street again, after the attempt. I let one go at Ord Chandler an' missed him an' hit Nash. Then Nash got knocked right off the horse by a second one."

"From you?."

"No. I'm more'n ninety per cent sure it was from Augie Telfer. Anyway, he didn't get up."

Macken was scraping slowly at his rough-whiskered jaw. "Yeah, well, I do hear there's some hard boys come into this town an' it turns out the name o' one o' *them* is Nash, an' he's said to be kin to the one that got nailed in Warbeck. Brother. Younger brother."

After a brief pause Gowan said

108

evenly, "That's interesting, Ed, but I'm not here for a fight with this Nash or anybody else that might have an axe to grind. I'm here for one reason, to talk with my wife."

"So be it," Macken said, "but I had to give yuh due warnin'. A lot o' folks know you've come here."

"Likely he'll not know of me or get to hear of me."

"Don't bank on that," Macken said at once. "This dump's crawlin' with real helpful citizens. If he don't know yet, he will soon."

"Then I'll have to watch my step," said Gowan, "an' my back."

It turned out to be a prophetic remark.

Gowan had plenty of time to fill in before he could make a second attempt to talk with his wife, and when eventually he emerged from Macken's office, and not wishing to wander through the town, he headed at once for the back-street where his hotel stood. He had no way of knowing it but he was doing this some twenty minutes after Nash, coming back into the Red Deuce, a smoky place that was well-attended for the afternoon hour, had rejoined Staples, Bascom and Brophy.

All four had been drinking steadily for a couple of hours and other patrons were steering well clear of them. The scuff-booted, hard-staring, dirty men had been recognized for what they were from their first appearance.

Nash slumped down again onto his chair, at a table that by now was a forest of bottles and glasses.

"Jes' heard," said Nash in his hard, slightly nasal voice, "that bastard Gowan from Warbeck's here."

Brophy set his glass down. "Well, I'll be god-damned."

"Where is he?" Staples asked, his small eyes blinking at Nash.

"One o' them rat-houses off Main, one right alongside some storehouse called Ostler's."

Staples belched. "Too good a chance

to miss. Somethin' to be put right. Settled."

Nash nodded. "I'd know that bastard, too, if I seen 'im. Come across pictures, at the time, in 'papers."

"Me too," said Staples. "Me too."

That was why, with his ramshackle hotel in sight, on an otherwise garbage-littered and weedy street, Gowan suddenly became aware of them, all four, two putting in an appearance up ahead of him, two a little distance behind him.

Gowan, loose-limbed, as though he cared nothing about it, kept striding on, and whilst he knew that up against four, whatever they chose to do, he did not stand a spit-in-hell chance, the fact that he was coming along without the merest check gave him at least a few moments to puzzle them, and it was in fact enough to bring him within thirty feet of the two who had come to a stop now, ahead of him. There was no doubt in his mind that this would be Nash's crowd, Macken's prediction having come joltingly true, but there was no possibility of retreat for he could hear the quickening of boots from those behind. Only when Nash spoke did Gowan himself stop, but by now he had closed to within fifteen feet of them.

"This is the bastard."

"Doubtless you'll be Nash," said Gowan.

"Ain't no doubt at all," said Nash nasally. Small hairs on the back of Gowan's neck tingled as from not far behind him he heard the cocking of a pistol. Well, if they were about to kill him there was not a goddamn' thing he could do about it, but he did have a fleeting, if useless regret that it would come to pass in such a dirty, no-account, fly-blown place as this. Yet, half drunk or not, maybe Nash still had enough wit to realize what a killing might cost him in the long run, when his true purpose was locating the money, for he gave a slight shake of the head, then came pacing on alone towards Gowan. "Been a while gittin' to it, you an' me, but it had to come sometime."

"No doubt," said Gowan. He still could not win, even if there was no shooting. Then he sensed as much as heard one of them moving closer in behind him, and he made a sudden step to one side.

The down-whipping long barrel of the pistol, intended to be laid across the back of his head, now only brushed heavily against his right shoulder, and, pivoting, Gowan then swung his right fore-arm back in a powerful arc to catch the man — Bascom it was — across the face and send him staggering away, almost tangling with the round-faced Brophy who was with him.

Nash, however, now closed the distance remaining between them, swinging a savage punch as he came which, although Gowan did his best to evade it, slammed across his left cheekbone and drove him to his knees. Then one of Nash's boots came thumping solidly into Gowan's ribs, sending a fiery poker of pain through him as he went rolling away.

Struggling to a half crouch, Gowan raised his thick forearms to ward off Nash's following blows, and rising, managed to jab at the man's face to jolt him, surprising him, checking his advance; but others were there then, enveloping Gowan, sharp, grunting blows catching him, sending lights bursting across his vision, the warm stickiness of his own blood now on his face and down his shirt. Overwhelmed, Gowan fell.

Standing over him, they would have systematically kicked him into unconsciousness, perhaps even to death, but even Gowan, the daylight fading from his sight, was aware of the gunshot; and when, sluggishly, he rolled over and tried propping himself away from the sandy, weedy earth, although he could not quite manage to rise, he knew that the men were no longer crowding him and kicking at him.

Shaking his head, spraying droplets of blood, blinking, trying to clear his vision, he found that he was now on hands and knees, senses still reeling, pain in his face and head and around his ribs; and he could hear voices calling, but could not yet make sense of what they were saying. Just how long he remained in that dog-like, head-hanging attitude he did not know, but his next awareness was of a voice he thought he ought to recognize, saying, "C'mon, Bob. Time to git on your hind legs." Ed Macken. Someone else with him. Bob Sloane, one of Macken's deputies, as it turned out.

Then Nash's voice was saying, "This ain't no way your quarrel, sheriff. This is strictly 'twixt me an' that goddamn' back-shootin' bastard there."

"In this county, an' on any one o' these streets," said Macken, "it allers turns out to be my business. Back off. Are you Nash?" Though Nash, still staring malevolently at Gowan, did not answer, Macken took it as read, surveying him and the ragged and dirty men who were with him. But Macken was well aware that this brawl was indeed only one of many he had had to break up as a matter of course. The fact that this one might have deeper reasons than most of the others, that at the centre of it was a lawman from a neighbouring county, was somewhat unusual; but even so in a town such as Gaspard it was scarcely an arrestable offence. Keeping the law wherever it was that you happened to be in this raw country was often a rough and demanding business. Sometimes it turned out you were ahead; sometimes, somebody was on the wrong end of a beating. "Get gone," Macken said to Nash, "out o' my sight, an' take these turkeys with you. Piss on the peace one more time an' I'll come on in with all my deputies, an' one way or another yuh'll be in the cage to cool off, an' then on your way out o' the county."

Oddly enough, the short fight and

the coming of the law and even the gunshot fired in the air by Macken seemed not to have attracted undue attention. Sure, at a distance there were a few questioning faces but no crowd had gathered.

With a show of brooding reluctance, unwilling to be seen as being pushed by anybody, Nash and his companions began moving away, but from time to time were looking back.

"We'll come up with yuh ag'in," Nash promised Gowan, "here or in Warbeck. That's a promise, mister."

Sloane was helping Gowan to his feet. "Boy," Sloane said, "they sure enough set out to work yuh over, Mr Gowan."

Only minutes after Gowan, insisting that he would be all right, had also gone slowly away, Macken, standing in the doorway of his office, watched as Stace Culley and Allie Joubert went by on ambling horses, Allie looking trim and somehow younger in snug-fitting blue shirt and tan, divided riding-skirt and a flat-crowned, wide-brimmed grey hat. Macken's pouched eyes followed the pair of them all the way along Main.

Macken's eyes were not the only ones watching the casually chatting riders going by. A number of people were studying them, among them, having just stepped out of a barber-shop, Arne Malpass, feeling a surge of anger and jealousy, turning away sharply though lest someone should see and read his expression.

Further off still, at an upstairs window, an executive of the S-W railroad also looked speculatively at the two of them; and at his elbow a man from the US Treasury watched too, in brooding silence.

And Nash saw them, but his whole attention was fastened on Allie Joubert, his eyes slitted, a puffed-up bruise beneath one of them where Gowan's big fist had found its mark. Nash considered he had sure not done with Gowan yet, not by a long shot; and he had not yet even started with Allie Joubert.

A couple of hours later, thoroughly if painfully washed, salve on a cheekbone and on split lips, walking slowly and stiffly, mainly because of the pain in his ribs, Gowan came to a lamplit side door of the Gaspard House Hotel and asked the skinny man in the monkey jacket who answered his knocking, for Mrs Gowan.

Gowan, seen in early evening under the porch lantern, must have presented a fearsome spectacle what with his size and his obvious injuries, and the man's face took on an expression of grave uncertainty.

"I'll wait right here," Gowan said slowly, "while you go find out if Mrs Gowan is there. Tell her that her husband, Sheriff Gowan is here."

The man's suspicious eyes swept Gowan's shirt and open jacket, perhaps seeking a badge, and finding none he looked even more unsure, but at length gave a brief nod and closed the door.

At first Marion stood stock-still at the sight of him, but then she said, "You'd better come on in."

Gowan took his hat off and followed her, closing the door after him, and she led him up carpeted stairs to her room. Not until they were there did she turn to look at him again and he did not have to wait for her to speak to know that all the old doubts and hesitations and fears must have come flooding back at the sight of the ugly, raw marks on him, the indisputable marks of violence. When she spoke, what she said confirmed it. "Nothing changes. Nothing at all, wherever you go."

Gowan, at a low ebb, did not want to get into a position of having to defend himself, much less offer her pallid excuses, but he felt he had to give some kind of explanation.

"One of the men shot at Warbeck when they tried for the jail was named Nash. His brother's turned up here with a few other hard boys in tow. They heard I was here. I didn't know

120

about them or about this other Nash. That's the straight of it."

She had half raised one slim hand, her eyes closed for an instant.

"Bob. Bob, you must know I've heard it all before or things very much the same. I'm truly sorry you've been hurt but since I've come here to this place, been by myself, one thing that I *have* known is peace of mind. I've been fully occupied. I've had no time to brood on the past, and the effect has been like a heavy weight being lifted off me. Believe me, Bob, I'm not placing *blame*. It's not that. I'm simply saying what I know, how I feel. As matters stand I truly don't believe I could go back to the way things were, if that's what you've come here to ask me."

Gowan could not have denied that it was a heavy blow to his hopes. What she had just said seemed to have removed at a single stroke all of the persuasions he had been going over in his mind during the weeks leading up to this visit, persuasions that had seemed so compelling when he had formed them in his head.

"I'd hoped we could get everything out in the open," he said, "by starting to talk again. That's all I was seeking, a chance to talk. We didn't throw all those good years away, Marion, we let 'em just *fade*, until they got out of reach. It didn't seem right then an' it doesn't now. I'm ready to admit faults, an' I know there are plenty."

"It's not a matter of *faults*, not in the way you mean." She turned away abruptly, then crossed to the darkening window. "I don't want to quarrel with you, Bob. Let's just leave it for now. Let's give it a little more time."

It was not what he wanted but he said, "I'd like to stay on in Gaspard until we can get something agreed." He knew he might be pushing it some now.

"Agreed. Maybe that's too much to hope for. I *am* sorry, Bob, but I do have to say it."

"I'd rather not leave it like that."

"All right. All right." She came away from the window, her face quite still, serious, and if he had hoped to read warmth there he would be disappointed. "Let's talk again tomorrow. About this same time. Go get some rest, maybe see a doctor." *He looked the way he'd looked so often in Warbeck.*

Watching him as he left, quietly closing the door after him, she felt a cold shudder run through her as though whatever Nemesis had followed him to this place had now reached out and touched her too, with chill, cadaverous fingers.

8

THE short but vicious encounter with Nash and his drink-fired cohorts had been the very last sort of incident that Gowan had been seeking. Such a confrontation could not have come at a worse time for him and indeed he now thought that it might well have influenced in the worst possible fashion the outcome of his visit to Gaspard. Still aching deeply from the blows he had taken, his lower lip freshly afire after a doctor named Booth had inserted three stitches.

Marion Gowan, too, was both saddened and disturbed. One part of her rued the judgemental way in which she had spoken to Gowan. She had had no desire to turn their first real meeting in such a long while into any kind of confrontation, but somehow the unexpected sight of Gowan's injuries, the awful evidence of violence, when it had appeared before her, had triggered quick words which, later, she thought would have been better left unsaid. Now, there was an irony. From a time in Warbeck when the most telling, the most destructive of their problems had been a dearth of talk, a loss of ordinary communication between them, to this sharp-edged rush of words with which she had greeted him tonight. So it was chiefly herself she now castigated, if silently, for not once had she expressed — much less demonstrated — any real concern for Gowan. *I'm truly sorry you've been hurt* had had an empty ring. All that she had seemed to convey was a concern for herself, for how it all had affected *her*; and for that she now felt a deep sense of shame. Clearly he had been at grave risk in a confrontation which, she quite believed, he had not sought. That he had come away from it with the injuries he had, and not near-crippling ones, was maybe due only to chance. A chill now settled over her again, but mixed with the remorse which she felt was the knowledge that, while she feared *for* him, she must also admit, again only to herself, that it was this very climate of uncertainty, of sharp danger, which had helped to drive them apart in the first place, and probably would continue to do so if they were to come together again. Violence, danger, fear were at the heart of everything that had beset them in their life together in the past.

At the East Hotel Brophy was again lying with the silk-smooth, coffee-coloured girl who could neither hear nor speak. Brophy could hear well enough, however, and what now came to his ears was Nash calling for him down the bare wooden passageway outside. Brophy, however, chose not to answer.

When Nash opened the door and booted it back, quivering, dust springing from it, Brophy at once took more interest, struggling to sit up among the ravaged bedclothes, in spite of the girl's two-armed, finger-locked efforts to restrain him, her smooth, bold breasts shaking.

"Yuh caught the goddamn' deaf sickness as well?" Nash enquired.

Brophy, recovering from surprise, was unfazed, exposing the girl's long left thigh and slapping it. "What she's short of in some parts she makes up fer in others."

Nash was in pants and blue-striped grey shirt, broad brown galluses over his shoulders. The side of his nose and the eye where Gowan's punch had caught him was red and swollen and he did not look to be in any mood to bandy words with Brophy or anybody else.

"Yuh git that dumb bitch peeled off yuh an' come on down. We been pissin' around here long enough."

"Goin' out to see Bob Gowan ag'in?"

"If that chance comes, I'll take it. No, what we got to talk about now is Mrs Allie Joubert."

"Ah," said Brophy, "we're right back to her."

"Bascom's keepin' an eye on her."

"That'll be two of 'em crowdin' her," said Brophy, "him an' that fancy faro-dealer."

"The hell with Culley. I got no business with him nor him with me."

Later in the day Allie Joubert went riding unhurriedly along the main street and eventually headed out of Gaspard. Alone. She had finished outstanding work and had easily prevailed upon Malpass to release her for the remainder of the day and his little eyes had followed her greedily as she put on hat and cape and left the office.

For Allie, this was a second, planned step. The first had been to be seen riding in and out of town in the company of Stace Culley; now the nudgers and whisperers could become accustomed to seeing her sometimes riding alone. Riding out, riding back. Then one day, perhaps not far into the future, she would simply ride out and not come back. That would be when she would find her own way to where the money was, and at first, simply to assure herself that it was there. Then away again, this time up to Fayette, not Warbeck, not anywhere near that man Gowan, and once in Fayette, acquire a strong pack-horse. After a time. Nothing rushed. She would not make that mistake, and draw unwanted attention to herself.

Culley did not like this, of course, this business of her riding out alone. Culley again. In spite of all that had happened she had still held back from confiding in him; in fact she had taken this opportunity — her intention to go riding — to indicate to Stace Culley, albeit in a gentle way, that no matter how close they had become, Allie Joubert was still her own woman, and a woman confident in her own ability to look after herself.

For his part Culley had said that he had seen enough of life in these rugged western lands to remain highly sceptical of that, but he had just as quickly seen that he would have no chance of dissuading her by wordy argument. The one thing he *was* able to do was to press upon her as a gift a small .41 calibre Hammond Bulldog pistol, a single-shot, rimfire weapon which was, he had assured her, most effective at close quarters.

"Stace, I'm not so sure I fancy the sound of close quarters," Allie had said wryly, "but I can see that you're concerned for my health. Thank you, Stace." But perhaps he had suspected that she had not really wanted the thing. She had been certain that she had not, for firearms of various kinds had worked devastation in Allie's life in recent times.

But she had accepted it and that had been that. On the particular afternoon she chose to head on out of Gaspard on her own, however, Culley was not even aware that she had actually departed; and such was the general activity in town that few other people were aware of it either. The sight of Allie Joubert riding by was no longer food for discussion.

So the sharp roofs and false fronts, the smoky atmosphere and the seemingly unending noise of Gaspard soon fell behind her, and although that was a certain relief to her, she had no intention of venturing too far today, knowing that there was at least some substance to Stace Culley's concerns for a woman who chose to ride out unaccompanied. A short, pleasant ride before supper was all that it was to be.

The reason that Stace Culley did not know about Allie's movements on that afternoon was that he had been to yet another of his discreet meetings with his superior from the Treasury and the regional manager of the S-W railroad. Both of these men were becoming, to say the least, somewhat querulous. Meares, the elder one, the bullish, nearly bald man from S-W, Culley had always been confident of handling. An overly simplistic man, not noticeably intelligent, Meares had come up through the S-W ranks probably by shouldering others aside, and though in the process of promotion becoming to some extent groomed, gave the impression of an entrenched belief that the most effective way to solve most problems was to swat someone over the hat with a pick-handle until all others read the message.

Dillon, on the other hand, as Culley knew, was of another kind entirely, his long, sad features more in keeping with those of some discontented cleric, an impression much strengthened by his wearing of quite sober attire; and his speech, in his velvety voice, was somehow more effective than all of Meares's hoarse-breathing bluster.

It was in fact Dillon of the dark, grey-threaded, brushed-back hair who, apparently less convinced, now, of the delicate line Culley must tread than he seemed to have been at earlier meetings, said, "I have to tell you, Culley, that in my opinion this whole matter has dragged on quite long enough. For one thing, by now I would have expected Ulrich to have made some contact, at least given us some sign of his presence."

"If Ulrich rode directly to the ravine, not pushing things too hard, and made a camp there and started poking around," Culley observed, "he'd hardly have had time to do anything about that. And anyway, why would we want him showing up in Gaspard?"

"Time." Dillon isolated the word as though it had been the very one he had been waiting for and Culley was perfectly well aware that for Dillon, measures of time were laid off not in terms of minutes, hours and days, but purely in dollars and cents, and that such was the case became evident now as Dillon went dourly on. "Unfortunately, even in the Treasury, as you know, we do not have an inexhaustible supply of . . . time. The longer this phase is allowed to stumble on the more will our energies become dissipated." *Allowed*.

Culley almost said something he would later have regretted, but it was Meares, groping about in an inside pocket for a cigar, who said heavily and directly, "This Joubert woman *know* anything or not, Culley, in your judgement?"

Culley's long hands slid into his pants pockets. "If she does," he said carefully, "then so far I've not been able to find out what it is."

"You *have* questioned her?" Dillon asked silkily.

That did it for Culley. Senior to him or not, Culley rounded on him, hands now out of his pockets. "*Questioned? Of course I haven't questioned her. Excuse me, Mrs Joubert, but rumour has it you were very tight with that killer, that Jack Chandler who got hold of all that money and then got himself blown away in Warbeck. Now, did he happen to tell you where he'd hidden it?*"

"Culley, I find your tone and your

manner deeply offensive," Dillon said, his cadaverous face paler than ever, his eyes icy, his voice down almost to a whisper. "Kindly remember who you are and who I am."

Culley held his anger in, knowing that he might have come close not only to damaging his career but also to betraying the ambivalence of his feelings for Allie Joubert. And he had set out to do precisely what Dillon had been expecting him to do, to question her, albeit indirectly, and indeed that had been his sole purpose in getting close to her. But at that time, in the beginning, he had had no notion that his own feelings for her would deepen in the way that they had. Sure, she was an older woman, but a sensuously attractive one. No wonder men looked at her with such unvarnished hunger. There was just something *about* her, beyond her good looks, beyond the much-younger-woman silkiness of her skin, her beautifully-formed full lips or her large, almond eyes, something invisible but undeniably present, a spirit, a warmth, a vibrancy. Culley believed that even if Allie Joubert had been a woman of plainer features she would still have had this breath-shortening magnetism, for it had little to do with looks.

"I believe," said Culley slowly, "that Mrs Joubert is close to confiding in me, Mr Dillon."

Mrs Joubert. Both of the other men looked back at him, the bulky Meares, his cigar now alight and generating sweet blue smoke, the ascetic, fussy, too-well-dressed Dillon, as though they did not suspect that Culley was bedding her, uniting unspokenly in perpetuating an absurd pretence. *Use any means*, Dillon had said that to Culley at one time. Maybe the man really had been too stupid to realize all the possibilities which might arise from an instruction such as that.

"Well, with any luck at all," Meares mumbled, "your man, ah, Ulrich will come up with something anyway." But

Meares was still annoyed that he had not been told about this Ulrich right from the start.

Culley did not believe that to be the case any more and thought that Meares probably didn't either. A whole lot of people had gone into that ravine and searched and come away with only aching limbs and a fierce thirst. Culley, having given it a lot of thought, no longer believed that Jack Chandler's train-money was where everybody had assumed it to be. The fact that Chandler had been taken in that place proved nothing. Culley knew, too, that the Slane County sheriff, Bob Gowan, happened to be in town, and would have given a lot to talk with him about that whole affair, but Culley was resigned to the fact that as long as he was trying to work on Allie Joubert he could not take the added risk of going anywhere near Gowan. Having to meet covertly with Dillon and this dim-witted railroad man was risky enough if he was to preserve secrecy.

"I just wish you'd set up something more definite with your man Ulrich," Meares said, oddly unwilling to let that matter drop, and then he said, "I hear there was a set-to between that man Gowan an' some of the hard-noses in town."

"Gowan came off second-best," said Culley, "but Sheriff Macken stopped it before they actually kicked Gowan's head off."

Dillon fastened his attention on Culley. The Treasury man did not much care about Gowan or Macken or hard men come out of nowhere, but only about finding out, and quite soon, what Allie Joubert might know. But he did say, "If it should turn out that your Mrs Joubert in fact knows *nothing*, Culley, there will be questions asked, no doubt, about why it took so long to discover *nothing*."

This time Culley had his anger under firm control, though no doubt Dillon believed he could still detect evidence of it in the tautness of Culley's face.

"I'll make another attempt tonight," Culley said steadily, "to find out once and for all." His only wish was to know how he might go about it.

★ ★ ★

Beyond a string of skinny alders, following a faint trail, Allie Joubert was about a mile and a half out of Gaspard.

Over to her right, across broken, brush-pocked flats, the Fayette Hills, rich with pines on their lower slopes and with loftier firs above them, were throwing ever-lengthening shadows across the earth. In that direction, too, it was possible to see the haze of steam and smoke being thrown up by the Dolbeer donkey-engines, and a column of denser smoke rising from a great heap of burning sawdust; and on the relatively still afternoon air was carried the pulsating sounds of the engines and the thin, banshee-howling of the big circular saws. Malpass's lumber-camp, its unceasing activities eating whitely into the rich green of the Fayette slopes like some giant-jawed caterpillar.

Seeing and hearing the working of the distant mill spurred Allie's thoughts to the unlikeable and rather unsettling Malpass and his scarcely less repulsive wife, Hetty, a brooding, spiteful woman, watching Allie and no doubt fashioning in her busy mind absurd adulteries. Well, no matter, Allie thought, for quite soon she would be up and gone from that town, and it was now highly likely that when she did she would have no company. It would be a move involving enormous risks but she had not come as far as she had, armed with vital information from Jack Chandler himself, by being faint of heart.

Allie brought the livery-horse, a sturdy sorrel, down to a gentle trot, then drew it to a stop. She had now ridden out about as far as she wished to and would simply sit quietly for a few minutes, allowing the animal to take a breather, then set out again to return to Gaspard. The veriest whisper of a breeze had now come up and borne upon it was the penetrating smell of smoke, no doubt from the Malpass mill.

It was on this faint breeze, too, that she thought her ear caught a sound, not close at hand to be sure, but definite enough, and she turned her head to stare out across the brushy flatlands at her back. The clipped sound of a shod hoof striking stone. Allie sat quite still, listening. Nothing more. Half a minute went by and still nothing. None the less she slid her gloved hand into the deep pocket of her tan riding-skirt, feeling the presence of the blunt little single-shot Bulldog which she had not really wanted but had accepted from Stace Culley simply to appease him.

She waited, sitting still, for another couple of minutes before she turned the horse around and began heading back in the direction of the town. Suddenly she felt tense again and for the first time experienced a real niggle of doubt about the wisdom of venturing as far as she had on her first ride alone; and at every stride of the loping sorrel she felt the gathering of cold sweat between her shoulder-blades. Someone else was indeed out here, and not far away.

9

THEY had come to an agreement to set aside their previous tense exchange and to start over, albeit tentatively. What at their previous meeting had been confrontational had now transformed itself into a strange, awkward reticence as between two people who were little more than mere acquaintances, yet they were not as distant as once they had been in Warbeck.

They agreed, also, because the evening was not yet chill, to walk together while they talked. After all, that was the important thing, to be able to exchange their views, confront their problems without acrimony, to explore if they could the true reasons for their earlier discontent and at least make some kind of start in trying to resolve them.

"No promises," Marion had warned, however. "No commitments to be given on either side. Not yet, Bob. I believe it's much too soon for that. To reach that point might take several talks. Maybe it won't even be possible. We shall have to see."

"Agreed," Gowan had said. Much less than he had been seeking, yet right now more than he had dared to hope for.

Still on Main, at the corner of the rubbishy street where Gowan's hotel was, they paused, uncertain of the direction to take, when Gowan's attention was caught by a man who had just emerged from the office of the county sheriff and was still in conversation with someone standing inside. The early lamplight was washed across the features of the man and his attire, and Gowan said to Marion, "That's Stace Culley up there?"

"Yes, I think that's his name. He's a professional gambler, so I hear, in one of the saloons."

People were criss-crossing the street, and soon their view of Culley was lost, but a short time later, when they were strolling by the jail, they saw Macken alone in the doorway, apparently ready to step out on the street. He touched the brim of his hat to Marion, while to Gowan he said, "Stace Culley come by in a hell of a lather. Seems he's lost track of Mrs Joubert."

Very quickly, sensing from Macken's tone that this might be something that he and Gowan had been discussing before — for Gowan had told her that he had called on Macken — Marion shot a quick glance at her husband.

Gowan, if he noticed, gave no sign. "You mean *he* can't find her?" he asked.

"That's what he claims. Seems she went along to a livery an' got the horse she's been ridin' lately an' headed off out o' Gaspard. Told the liveryman she'd not be gone more'n an hour. That was mebbe four hours ago."

Gowan did not have to think about it for long. "If Allie Joubert does know where Jack Chandler put that money, maybe she's headed away to try to lift it." Even as he said it, however, Gowan was unconvinced, for surely whoever did get at the money would need a pack-horse to move it far.

"It's a possibility," Macken said, not convinced either. "But if she ain't, then ridin' out alone fer no reason wasn't the best idea she coulda had. From what he said, Culley told her that, even give her one o' them little Bulldogs." Macken rubbed at his jaw and sniffed and looked up at a sky that was beginning to be picked out with pale stars. "Give her the chance o' one shot, a Bulldog."

Gowan then said, "Could be any reason, Ed. Maybe the horse went lame, or maybe she's been thrown. Whatever it is, are you planning on going out to look?"

"If I do, it sure won't be 'til sun-up,"

146

said Macken. Then, "Culley reckons she'll likely have headed out across the flats where she's been before, when Culley was along."

Hardly had Macken said this than Gowan, looking beyond him, fastening his attention on a particular horseman coming along Main, a figure caught from time to time in flung lamplight, made a brief hand movement and said, "Culley's not about to wait 'til sun-up."

Macken and Marion Gowan both half turned to look. Sure enough, the neatly-dressed faro-dealer, now wearing a stiff-brimmed, dove-grey hat and a loose denim jacket over his white shirt rather than his frock-coat, was riding by looking neither to left nor right, completely absorbed, it seemed, with his own thoughts and purpose. Though he could not be certain, Gowan got the fleeting impression of a pistol in a saddle-holster. All three watched until the bobbing rider finally vanished into shadows where no lamps burned.

Walking away with Marion, Gowan was at once aware of a new tautness in her attitude and they had not gone more than a dozen paces before she said in a low but firm voice, "Was that it then, Bob? Is that the real reason you've come here, because of the money from the train? Because that woman Joubert is here and might *know* something? Is that what's still eating at you?"

Even in the gloom the shock must have shown and he stopped, turned and took her gently by her slim shoulders. "No, Marion, that's *not* it. That wasn't why I came to Gaspard. I came to talk with *you*, no other reason."

It was impossible for Gowan to know whether she believed him or not, for while her tone was moderate, she said, "But not finding that money from the train, you still see that as a personal failure, don't you, Bob? And you will, until somehow *you* are involved in finding it."

It would have been utterly useless

for him to deny at least part of it, for he knew she understood him and the things that moved him better than anyone else. "Any lawman, anywhere, would want to finish off something like that, all those deaths that happened because of it."

She was disposed to say very little more as he walked her back towards the Gaspard House, knowing without even asking, that she would want to talk no more tonight on the subject they had set out to discuss.

A short time later, when he moved his face down to brush her cheek, she turned her own cool face away. It was as though, no matter what he might say to her now, more damage had been done, damage that might not readily be repaired. Jack Chandler and all the other dead from the train and from the break-out at Warbeck had reached up from the darkness of their graves to touch him yet again.

★ ★ ★

Allie Joubert, letting the horse stretch out, was now in full flight, for there was no doubt that the men who were out here had been looking for her and had at once, upon sighting her, set out towards her.

Now they were calling sharply to each other as they rode, the sounds like the sharp yapping of dogs, three riders, maybe four, and to her mounting alarm she soon saw that they had contrived to cut across the line-of-ride that would have led her directly back towards Gaspard, so that now she was being driven at an angle that would take her further away.

The afternoon light was fading, the shadows of the High Torres and the Fayette Hills folded below them, having spread far out across these flats, and it would not be long before the night came down. The hired horse that Allie was on was barely above average, if anything with a little too much condition on, and she feared that before much longer, going at

150

this urgent pace, it must soon begin labouring under her.

Who these men could be she did not know, for they had been too far off to see their features, but there had been an immediate and unmistakable menace in the way in which, the moment they had seen her, they had acted as though they had recognized *her*, and were out to do her harm. Too late, as she had urged the sorrel to a full gallop, the recollection of Stace Culley's warnings had come back to her.

Clusters of lethal thorn-brush were slipping by in a blur, sometimes seeming to lunge at her as she sent the straining animal weaving in and out, dust rising in a misty trail behind her, the woman now driven by a mounting terror, the quick unnerving yapping of the chasing riders still clearly audible to her. Frantically quirting the stretching horse, not daring to look behind her, Allie bore onwards, aware that the animal was no longer moving anywhere near as willingly, and that the shouts of the men behind her were getting closer.

Desperately, Allie set about quirting the animal even more fiercely, gloved hand whipping back and forth, concentrating only on riding hard, instinctively drawing upon all her girlhood experience, knowing that she must take the chance that a quickly-tiring horse would be more likely to stumble and throw her. And as she rode she was trying to edge back in the direction which would take her towards Gaspard. Thundering through slightly thickening brushlands, she was sweating and covered in fine dust now, her breath fiery in her throat.

How long she managed to keep the lathered horse to that furious pace she did not know, but eventually she realized that whatever happened she must ease up on it now, give the animal a breather or risk it collapsing under her. If the worst came to the worst she would have to dismount and slip away among brush to try to hide from them.

So Allie eased the sweat-rimed sorrel down to a canter, then trotted it to a halt and it stood, head hanging, blowing, sides heaving as she slipped to the ground and stood looking back the way she had come, listening for the sounds of the other horses.

Almost half a minute had gone by before she was able to convince herself that there were no sounds whatsoever to be heard other than those being made by her own distressed animal. She moved to the horse's head, began smoothing a gloved hand down its long nose, murmuring to it. She was tired and felt grimy and was still having to draw in long, restoring breaths herself as she waited, still listening. It was true. There were no other sounds out there. They had given up, or they, too, had stopped to rest their horses and to listen. The dust that her own frantic ride had raised was now no more than a faint mist hazing over the darkening brushlands.

Still she waited as the minutes went

sliding by, still having to reach for breath, but the pounding of her heart was at last settling down. Only then did she again remember the small pistol in the pocket of her skirt and she withdrew it, looking at the stubby ugliness of it. She wondered if, had it come to the point, she would really have tried to use it, even tried to kill one of them. Allie took a long, still unsteady breath and slid the Bulldog back down in her pocket.

★ ★ ★

Collis came stepping into the office. Macken was back in there, having been out around the streets for a while, looking here and there, trying the door handles of darkened buildings. Now, however, he was about ready to leave and go home. Collis, his hat pushed back on his head, turned one of the chairs back to front and sat down, arms resting on the back of it.

"I hear that Joubert woman that

works for Malpass is missin'," he said, "an' they reckon Stace Culley's gone out to look for her."

"I saw Culley headin' out," Macken said, rubbing a hand slowly over his face. "He'd been along here, earlier, soundin' off about it."

"She was on a hired horse, so they say," said Collis. "Mebbe it throwed her." His round face was impassive as he sat staring at Macken.

"Mebbe so," said Macken. He was no more convinced of that than when Gowan had said it. Then, "What do yuh know about Stace Culley?"

Somewhat caught off guard by the question, Collis at first wondered if this was to be a lead-up to some criticism of the time he liked to spend at the tables up at the Red Deuce. Macken — rather strangely, Collis thought — disapproved, but so far had not actually raised the matter. "Come in from out o' state," Collis said. "But from where, he didn't say." He left it like that.

Macken said, "In my time I seen a lot o' fellers in his line o' work. They come an' they went. A few didn't git to live to old age." It was said ruminatively, but his tone was firmer when he added, "Your Mister Culley, he don't ring true."

To steer well away from footing that was suddenly uncertain, Collis said, "He's real tight with Allie Joubert." And he thought, *lucky bastard*.

"Yeah," said Macken. "It's why he's jumpin' up an' down now."

Then Collis surprised Macken. "That Nash that was up at Maggie's, him an' them other three boys, they've all lit out. Good riddance."

Macken sat quite still, staring at him, leathern face a mask, saying nothing for a while. Then, "When? When did they go, an' when did yuh find that out?"

Collis, sensing now that there was something much more in the question, shifted uncomfortably on the chair. "Earlier on."

"How *much* earlier on?" There was

an edge to Macken's voice and when Collis did not answer right away, Macken asked, "An' where did yuh come by that piece o' news, the Deuce or Maggie's."

"Some boys that had been at Maggie's come in the Deuce. An' Gus Greene was in." This was a man from a livery. "They rode on out a few hours back. Well, it was afore sundown."

Macken's heavily-bagged eyes regarded the deputy sombrely. He seemed on the point of saying something else, but in the event did not. Yet Collis had become well aware of the critical note riding on Macken's sharp questions about Nash. And, *the Deuce or Maggie's*? Macken was reaching for his hat. In his surly voice, he said, "Give it another hour, then lock up." At the moment the cells were empty.

Macken put his sweat-stained hat on and went out, pacing along the boardwalk, like Gowan, slightly stooped in his tallness, an old dog on the prowl.

Allie Joubert gone and not come back. Stace Culley gone to look for her. Nash and his hard lot gone. Where? Maybe, he thought, as county peace-officer, he ought to feel mighty relieved to be shot of the lot of them and all the threads of rumour that seemed to have been trailing after them. Suddenly Macken, feeling older than he had felt in a good long while, also felt the need to talk with someone who would be at one with his own perspective, and he then wondered if Bob Gowan had gone back to his crummy hotel, and if so, if he might still be wakeful.

★ ★ ★

It was near moonrise.

For close to ten minutes Allie Joubert had been walking, leading the nodding sorrel, unwilling to remount until she felt sure that the animal had in some measure got its wind back. Above her the heavens were scattered with faint stars. Presently she stopped and patted the horse's neck lightly, then moved to the near stirrup and swung up, leather creaking.

Allie walked the horse away, bit-chain clinking. Her own body had cooled but she felt grimy, sweat-dried. The sooner she got back to Gaspard and into a tub the better; and ruefully she wondered if she ought to make any sort of confession about this incident to Stace Culley, or simply keep her embarrassment about it strictly to herself. Well, she would make a decision about that when the time came; and by tomorrow she might see it all in a different light.

Presently she believed she could detect a certain brightness in the sky that was not the rise of the moon, but marked the still-invisible town of Gaspard. With a feeling of immense relief she urged the horse in that direction.

When, soon after, she came at a canter into a sizeable clearing among the brush, she hauled up in alarm and confusion. They were here, waiting for her, two sitting motionless horses near the middle of the open space and one at either side.

Allie, an awful dread clutching at her middle, brought her alarmed horse to a dead stop, the sorrel's head tossing, tail flicking.

"Christ," Nash said, not loudly but clearly enough, "we was gittin' around to thinkin' yuh'd never git here, Allie."

When they moved they closed on her so quickly that when one of them — Staples — arrived on her right-hand side, it was his horny fingers which seized her small wrist just as she was getting the little Hammond Bulldog clear. Staples ripped the weapon from her and flung it away.

They came crowding around her and she could smell their rank odour on the night air.

"Well," Nash said softly, "that was a surprise. Yuh might easy have done damage to some party with that thing, Allie. Never mind, we can't sit around here jawin' half the night. We got to git on the move."

Knowing there was no hope, she still had to say, "You've got no right to stop me. None at all. Anyway, by now I'll have been missed."

"Yeah?" said Nash. "Who by? That faro prick from the Deuce? C'mon, we're movin'."

"Where? Where to?" She could no longer keep her voice under control.

"Off'n these here goddamn' flats fer a start," Nash said, "to the Fayettes. An' then we'll build oursel's a little camp, Allie, an' we'll talk about you an' Jack Chandler an' all that *dinero* from that train, that nobody never did find."

"You'll be wasting your time," Allie said, "whoever you are."

"Nash," Nash said, "is my handle, an' these boys is Mister Staples, Mister Bascom an' Mister Brophy, an' I beg to differ, we'll by no means be wastin' our time, ma-am. By no means. We want to know a couple o' things an'

161

we want to know 'em right soon. Tonight, an' from you." Nash thrust his foul-breathed face close to her. "So jes' as soon as we git to where we're goin' an' git oursel's a fire lit, yuh might jes' as well let it all out, Allie, fer if yuh don't, then yuh ain't gonna be able to stand the pain. Pain like yuh never thought possible."

10

CULLEY, now that he was out on the flats, moving through the brushlands, did not know where the hell to begin looking, but wanted to dismiss any thought that this search he had set out on was, for that reason, sheer folly. He had come in the same direction taken when riding with Allie, the only frail thread of logic he had to work with.

Another matter was beginning to niggle persistently at Culley. At his last meeting with the humourless Dillon he had come close to losing his temper, something which would no doubt be remembered within the Treasury at some future time. Now he was committing another headstrong act, if anything worse than the first. Without even consulting Dillon he had headed impulsively out of Gaspard in an attempt to locate Allie Joubert. As Dillon would see it, he had allowed emotion to cloud his judgement and that would be certain to find no favour at all with the unappealing yet highly influential Dillon.

None the less Culley pressed on, pausing only occasionally to sit the horse quietly for a few minutes, listening, hoping for some sound, some call perhaps which would bring him quickly to her. For the moment, finding her was all that was concerning him, assuring himself that she had come to no real harm. The rest he would have to deal with as best as he could when the time came. It no longer mattered to Culley that she might well have been involved in some way with the Chandlers. From the moment that he had set eyes on Allie Joubert he had been strongly affected by her, and every day that had passed since then had seen the grip that she had on him grow tighter, so that he had taken to reminding himself more often of

164

the true purpose of his gaining her friendship.

After an hour of riding Culley drew the horse to a halt again, this time to spell the animal; and he dismounted. The night was starry and cool now and almost windless. Away to his right as he had been riding, he could discern the dark bulk of the Fayettes, the rise of the High Torres behind them, and off in that direction there came from time to time a wavering glow that he realized would be the constantly-burning, small hill of sawdust at Arne Malpass's mill which, during daylight hours, showed as a dirty smear against the sky.

Presently, perhaps sooner than was prudent, Culley remounted. The sense of folly in venturing out here at night came to him afresh, and ruefully he had to concede that the sober-faced Macken had probably had it right when he had said that if he did anything at all it would not be until sun-up. It seemed indisputably reasonable when compared with his own act, driven by emotion rather than good sense, in venturing out here by night.

Having come as far as he had, however, Culley now felt a reluctance simply to turn around and go back to Gaspard, and thereupon he decided to carry out a wide sweep that would take him nearer to the Fayette Hills then back to town in time to talk to Macken once more, to swallow his pride and organize a more disciplined search tomorrow. He grasped the butt of the Smith and Wesson pistol in its saddle-scabbard to assure himself that it was still firmly in place and turned the horse towards the dark Fayettes.

Culley had been heading in that direction for upwards of half an hour, hope receding with the passing of each minute, and he was about to veer away to take him angling back towards Gaspard when suddenly his attention was caught and he hauled up on the reins causing the horse to throw up its head and go skitter-stepping sideways, snorting and blowing. It was a moment or two before he got the animal properly under control. There, towards the hills, in fact in what he knew to be rougher, more broken terrain at the foot of that folded country, was what might have been, but for its low position, a winking star.

Culley blinked and concentrated, for whatever it was it seemed to be fading, then brightening. Too far south, he thought, to be anything to do with Malpass's sawmill, and anyway he could still discern the ruddy glow of that, he reckoned, much farther off.

Culley at once got the horse on the move again, knowing now that what he could see was a camp-fire, appearing and almost disappearing because of distance and perhaps branches moving across his line of sight. Allie? Maybe. It could be anybody, cowmen perhaps the most likely. Yet if it *was* Allie, then perhaps the horse *had* gone lame and somehow she had managed to get a fire started to wait out the cold hours of darkness. Maybe.

Culley now had to curb his rising excitement, not allow his hopes to build too much. He kept his attention on that small wavering light, moving inexorably towards it, aware, as he drew nearer, that the rougher country hereabouts was stonier, more dangerous, with small, unexpected upthrusts of rock to be wary of.

Right enough it was a camp-fire, but there was something odd about this place, so that with a hundred yards still to go Culley again stopped his horse. The camp, whoever had made it, was not completely out in the open, and this no doubt was the reason that the fireglow came and went as the angle of his approach had occasionally altered as he avoided obstructions. And a sound had been coming to him as he had been riding, one that he had taken to be the high keening of some nocturnal bird, but now in comparative stillness it came to him that what he had been hearing was no bird-sound. Indeed it was thin and high-pitched, but there was another element to it, coming and going, something harsh, and in its strangeness, nerve-stringing. The sound diminished, then came again more strongly, beginning in a low register, building quickly, soaring, breaking to raggedness, falling to sobbing and silence, and it was with a sudden chilling realization that brought breath gasping from him, that drained the very strength from his limbs, that Culley knew this was in fact the sound coming from some human being, venting to the unresponsive night some hell-fashioned agony, shrieking disjointed words that now began hammering at Culley.

Afterwards Culley did not remember the act of hitching the horse nor feeling the brush that clawed at him as he did it. He did not recall lifting the pistol from its saddle-scabbard. Culley could not at first interpret some of the other sounds that came to him as he first went walking forward, then jogging in and out between rocks and brush, towards the clearing where they were, his head feeling as though a steel band had been tightened around it, sounds that were like some kind of maniacal incantation rising about the dog-yapping of the men, sounds that were then recognizable as names, places, shrieked repeatedly to the night.

Culley's throat was burning as he ran strongly towards a camp-site he could now see fully, where the forms of crouching men were, where a whitely-naked woman was, Allie Joubert, and even as he got to within twenty yards of the place the scene that opened before him was a tableau from the very Pit itself, one man locking her arms behind her, one at either foot to spread her, one, Nash, cloth wadded around one end of a picket-pin held in a gloved hand, the other end of the pin cherry-red from the fire, squatting between her legs, no doubt whatsoever what it was he was again about to do to her.

Careless of the odds, in a rage beyond reason, almost demented, a cry that seemed scarcely human tearing from his throat, Culley, having momentarily halted, such was the horror of the scene revealed in the firelight of that benighted place, started forward again, the big Smith and Wesson swinging up even as the glow-lit faces under their wide-brimmed hats all now turned in his direction.

Staples, who was the one holding the woman's arms, was the first to make a move, releasing her, then making to draw his pistol, but as soon as the man was far enough away from Allie, Culley, in an acrid waft of gunsmoke, shot him, and in a series of curious lurching, bobbing movements, and crying out, Staples went crabbing away into the shadows and fell down there somewhere, out of sight.

Nash, already straightening and rising to his full height, the hand holding the pin that had become an awful instrument of torment raised above his head, then hurled it towards the advancing Culley, the still-glowing thing winking past him by no more than a couple of inches, so close in fact that Culley felt the brief heat of its passing.

Again Culley fired loudly but missed completely.

Round-faced Brophy, in the act of drawing, was yelling *"Gimme room!"* then fetching a long-barrelled pistol up.

Bascom, to make himself a smaller target, was diving to the ground.

Nash, a pistol now lifting in his hand, was however making no attempt to bring it to bear on Culley but pointing it at the writhing woman, and roaring, *"Back off!"*

Whether or not Culley had been recognized by them was unclear but when he saw what Nash was doing he pulled up short and then began retreating, not knowing if Allie Joubert would in any case survive what she had endured, but realizing that had he continued towards them she would most surely have been shot at once.

A deeply internal moaning noise was coming from Allie now, the sound as from a dreadfully hurt animal, and further off, in the anonymous gloom, Staples was gasping, "Jesus! Help me! Help me!"

Culley, stumbling away into his own shadows, seeking cover, saw the flick of flame as one among them, Brophy perhaps, let blast at him and a fire-rod sliced into Culley, spinning him around, sending him to his knees, losing the Smith and Wesson, hearing someone yelling, "Got 'im! Got the bastard!" Then Culley, though in pain, was forcing himself to get up and go blundering through the darkness, raked by brush, stumbling over stones, falling and getting up, wanting to shriek in his throbbing pain, urinating uncontrollably, beyond shame, seeking only safety, the reality of his rashness underscored by the bad wound he had taken.

★ ★ ★

173

They had gone quietly to one of the smaller saloons on Main, Macken and Gowan, where there were now fewer customers gathered under the smoky lamps, a room rank with the stench of stale beer and where the floor was a kicked carpet of wet sawdust.

Macken already knew that there was a lot more on Gowan's mind than Allie Joubert and Stace Culley, but it happened to be those two they were discussing now.

"If Culley don't show up with her by first light," Macken said, "I'll send a couple o' my boys out to take a look around." He took a long drink of beer, then set the foam-flecked glass down. "Mebbe I shoulda moved earlier, asked Mrs Joubert a few questions."

"On rumour?" Gowan, seated on the other side of the grimy table, knew well enough what was going through Macken's mind. "Things always look a whole lot simpler later than they do at the start, Ed. You could say I should've watched what was going on in Warbeck

174

a lot closer than I did, questioned a lot more, stood with Allie when she was in that saloon, close to Jack Chandler, that sort of thing. I've been over all that in my mind, since."

The lone bar-dog, a narrow-faced, button-eyed man, clearly unsettled by their unexpected presence, was almost visibly relieved when, not long after, they finished their beers, stood up and left. The hour was now quite late.

Gowan was just about to head off towards the dingy side-street where his hotel was when Macken, staring beyond him up Main in the direction of the county jail, said, "What's this?"

It seemed that a single, saddled horse was at the tie-rail up there and several people were clustered near it. Presently a figure detached itself and began coming somewhat vaguely along the street as though uncertain what to do."

"Looks like one o' your boys," Gowan remarked.

Macken acknowledged that by calling

out, "Coll!" The oncoming man looked, then came jogging anglewise across the street towards them and began calling before he got to them.

"Stace Culley," Collis said. "He's been shot an' he looks pretty bad. Somebody went to git Doc Allen but couldn't find him."

"Then you go git Hurst," said Macken sharply. Hurst was the druggist. Collis went loping away.

Walking quickly, Macken and Gowan went along the street to the small gathering in front of the jail.

Collis had been right. Culley looked to be very far gone indeed. Macken motioned a man with a lantern to come closer, then said, "For what it's going to be worth, let's git him inside the jail." Men came forward to do it, Macken going on ahead to open up a cell so that the wounded man could be put on a cot.

Hurst the druggist, his little round steel-framed eyeglasses winking, a long coat over his night-clothes, arrived breathless and carrying a large leather bag.

Macken cleared everybody except this man and Gowan away from the cell, and to Collis who had come back with the druggist, said, "Make sure they stay out; there's nothin' more to see or do here."

Hurst did what he could, which was not much, saying that the doctor had had to go out to a homestead some twenty-five miles away. "But I doubt he could do much more in the circumstances. It's a real bad one. He's bleeding internally. God knows how he managed to stay on a horse."

Much of Culley's upper clothing had by now been cut away and the remnants lay in a bloodied heap on the floor of the cell. Hurst's long coat was blood-smeared, as were his spidery hands, though Culley's chest, on the left side where the wound was, had been cleaned with methyl alcohol, leaving an innocuous-looking blue-lipped hole where the lead had gone into him. But there was rich blood on his mouth that kept appearing between his pale lips and on his chin, and this Hurst no longer bothered wiping away.

Suddenly Gowan was struck by the similarity of this death-scene with another, in a Warbeck saloon, the brigand Jack Chandler dying, the doctor simply awaiting the end, Gowan there, the preacher murmuring, Allie Joubert wiping Chandler's bleached brow.

Macken, like Hurst, had given up on Culley but Gowan, influenced by personal memories, bent over the dying man, voice low, insistent, willing him to come back, even if only for a few moments, into a state of awareness. But Gowan was asking no consistent questions of that waxen, blood-streaked face, bizarre in the poor light of a lantern, but was in fact repeating, like some soft litany, a single name. "*Allie Joubert . . . Allie Joubert . . . Allie Joubert . . .*"

Voices were sounding at the street

door and Macken went through to find out why. Gowan was still bending over Culley.

Eventually Macken came back into the cell and with him was a long-faced, pale man in a town suit, the vest strung across with a silver watch-chain, hatless, a man who Macken introduced to Gowan as Mr Dillon. "Of the S-W railroad," Macken added, for that had been his belief.

Gowan straightened up, moderately surprised, not perceiving any natural connection between Stace Culley and the railroad.

"Is he still alive?" Dillon asked in his velvety voice, and he crossed to the cot to see for himself.

"Barely," said Gowan. "Seems he went out to find a woman named Allie Joubert an' came back with a bullet instead."

Hurst came wandering across again to give Culley, who was now breathing with a bubbling sound, another cursory look.

As though suddenly aware that his interest would seem, to say the least, odd, Dillon looked perhaps uncomfortably from Gowan to Macken and said, "I have to tell you that Mr Culley here is not quite what he represented himself to be. In fact he is (he almost said *was*) an investigator from the US Treasury. There is a second one in the area, gone to that ravine, a man named Ulrich. I happen to be from the Treasury, also, and they are both my men."

Macken's old, fierce eyes pinned Dillon and after the shortest of pauses he said, "Yuh're tellin' me that Treasury investigators has come here to this county, sniffin' around, an' kept the reg'lar county law in the dark about it?"

For the second time since he had arrived, the sober-looking Dillon appeared to be slightly discomfited, perhaps because in his job he was more accustomed to asking questions of others rather than being questioned.

"It was thought advisable to do it that way," he said, "all previous efforts to locate the money having failed."

"Thought advisable," Macken said ruminatively. How he might have developed that point was not to be known for the man lying on the cot suddenly made a deep, retching noise and dark blood came gushing out of his mouth, and when Hurst stepped closer again and looked, Culley's eyes had already glazed.

"Gone," Hurst said, reaching to close the lids.

Gone indeed was Stace Culley, bearing with him to eternity the hellish scene that he had witnessed out at Nash's camp, the reality of his own fumbling, agonizing retreat through the dangerous brush to where the horse was tied, of hearing their voices calling to each other, searching for him, of dragging his ravaged body into the saddle, and of hearing, too, far back of him as he headed the horse away, the last act, eventually, near that dreadful fire, the single gunshot that would have carried Allie Joubert out of her world of pain.

Macken, barely managing to hold his anger in, turned again to Dillon. "If he was your man, then his corpse is your corpse. The undertaker's name is Shawcross. My deputy'll show yuh where to find him. Jes' so long as what's left o' your man is out o' here tonight." Dillon, his face grey, for he seemed to have no stomach for the sight of blood, watched as Macken, Dillon and Hurst all walked out of the cell. Outside, to Gowan, Macken said, "I got me a place down yonder. There's half a bottle in the cupboard." When they got there, Macken, lighting a lamp, asked for the first time, "Nary a word about Allie Joubert?"

"Yeah," said Gowan. "It's just that I didn't think it was any business of that Treasury prick."

Macken fetched bottle and glasses. "So Culley spoke."

"Yeah, came back to himself for a

time, to her name. Not for long and real quiet. She's dead. Shot. An' Nash had been burnin' her. She told them where the money is, an' Culley heard. Black Canyon. A passage somewhere in Black Canyon, a cleft, a cave, something like that."

"Jesus. In there? That's one hell of a place, Bob."

"It's just possible," Gowan said, "when you come to think of it. Jack was a shrewd man, moreso by a long shot than Ord. A lot more than Pearce. We took Jack when he was in that ravine. Maybe he'd figured people would think, if he happened to be seen coming out, that would be where he'd put the sacks. Somewhere in the ravine. But they were another five, six miles into the High Torres. Jack was a good move ahead. Again."

"So Allie Joubert did know."

"Yeah, an' Nash burned her until he got to know too."

Macken said, "I'll take a posse out, but I'd prefer to keep it small." He stared at Gowan. "I'd appreciate yuh ridin' in it." Then he looked away abruptly, sensing that he was probably asking too much of the man; but Gowan, taking a drink, nodded.

"I'll come." And as though he might have thought some explanation necessary, he added, "When I said to Marion that I'd not come here to follow the money, I was telling the truth, an' it stands. But whatever Allie Joubert was or wasn't, she didn't deserve what Culley said happened to her, not at the hands of Nash or anybody. Even so, Culley was using her too. Some might well say that when she made up her own mind to get that money, that made her as bad as any of them at that train. So be it. In the finish, Culley did what he could but it wasn't soon enough to help her. So it's just that I'd like to be along when you do take Nash, an' whether or not the goddamn' money gets found."

"I'll drink to that," said Macken, and he did. But it did not in any way ease his resentment of Dillon.

"Two of the bastards. Culley an' that . . . who did he say? Ulrich. Both sniffin' around an' me none the wiser. After all yuh done, an' all we done from here, at that time. So they ain't heard from that Ulrich. By God, if Nash was up in that ravine when he come, I'd bet *nobody's* gonna hear from *him*. I might go take a look sometime, even though it is in Slane County."

"I did hear somewhere," said Gowan, "that Nash an' his boys arrived towing a pack-horse. Could be they acquired that from Ulrich."

Macken, though, was still filled with recriminations and self-doubts, saying that he could have and should have done much more. "Damn it, Bob, I sat on my ass up here listenin' to all that jawin' — does she know, don't she know? All that. An' then I did nothin'."

Again, this was the doleful song so familiar to peacekeeper Gowan, for he had sung it so often himself at other times and had even added new choruses.

Almost savagely Macken poured fresh drinks, slopping some.

"My guess is," said Gowan, "that Nash won't move 'til sun-up. Where he's got to go with this new knowledge of his is no kind of country for a night ride. Well, I'd not fancy it. Could be you'd gain by heading out a couple of hours before light, an' if you push things along you'll maybe even spot where his camp is."

Macken agreed with that. "We'll do it."

"Who'll go?"

"You, me, Collis, Bob Sloane. Four."

"Four," Gowan repeated. It sounded to him to be a touch too light. He had had bitter experiences while riding at the head of small posses, not least among them the one he had taken out of Warbeck in pursuit of the bandits who had robbed the South-Western. He said, "No citizens to be deputized?"

Macken tossed his drink back,

grimaced, shook his head. "Never could watch two ways at once."

There was something in that, as Gowan had silently to concede. The memory of a young man, one of his own Warbeck posse, mortally wounded while he, Gowan, had been fully occupied in getting in close to Chandler, still haunted him; it had not yet been forgotten by a number of people in Warbeck. Or for that matter had his street pursuit of Jack Chandler, who finally had taken two bullets in the back.

Surprisingly, when Gowan came walking out of Macken's old frame house, Dillon of the Treasury was in the act of approaching it. Macken, having sunk a few with Gowan, stood blinking at Dillon for a moment or two as though he did not immediately recognize him. When he did, he said heavily, "What might *you* want, Mr Dillon?"

Dillon stopped, his long face no more than a pale wash in the night, and stood stiffly in front of Gowan.

"I wish to know," Dillon said in his whispery way, "if Mr Culley spoke to you about a Mrs Joubert. Particularly if he said anything when he came in, wounded."

"Ah," said Macken, "Mrs Joubert. Everybody seems to want to know about Mrs Joubert." He was breathing deeply and Gowan knew that the combination of drink and weariness and the knowledge of what had happened to Culley and to Allie Joubert and all the other business — as he would see it — under his nose, would likely have left Macken in a dangerous humour. "Mrs Joubert," Macken said deliberately and rather loudly, "is dead. She died in a real bad way, so we hear, an' all on account o' that goddamn' Treasury money."

Doggedly, Dillon asked, "How did you come by that information, Mr Macken?"

"In the finish, Mr Gowan here got it from a Treasury investigator that I didn't know nothin' about," Macken said. The dislike that Macken had formed for this man Dillon was palpable, but for all that, Dillon stuck grimly to his questioning.

"I must ask, then, if Mr Culley said anything else."

"What yuh want to know is if we found out where the money is."

"I have to ask it," Dillon said. "I have the right to know."

Feeling that Macken might be about to say something regrettable, Gowan said, "From what I could understand, Mrs Joubert was made to tell where the money's hidden. She was burned, internally, until she did."

Dillon's voice was lower and softer than ever when he repeated, "Burned?"

But it was not truly a question, and the implication of what he had been told was clearly not lost on Dillon who then said to Macken, "Do you intend seeking out the men responsible?"

"Of course I damn well do," said Macken.

"In that case," Dillon said, "I shall be accompanying you, Sheriff Macken, whenever you plan to go."

Macken was so taken aback that he could say nothing, his mouth falling open.

To Macken, Gowan said, "That money's been the magnet that's pulled in all sorts, the law, the scum an' the Treasury itself." And to Dillon, he said, "You'll have to be up an' ready to ride real early, Mr Dillon. In fact, I'd say it'd hardly be worth while going to bed."

"Right, Mr Dillon," Macken said then, partially recovering but his voice still rough with whiskey and anger. "I dunno how much ridin' yuh done, nor how much shootin' yuh done in your time, but I'll say this, in my posse I ain't nurse-maidin' no bastard whoever they might be. An' while you're ridin' in a posse o' mine, by God yuh'll take my orders or pay the price. Step out o' line an' I'll leave yuh out there afoot, an' if I do, yuh'll not last a day."

Hearing Macken get all this off his chest made Gowan think again about his ill-used Warbeck posse and a coldness settled on him. He had an almost overwhelming urge to go over to the Gaspard House to talk with Marion but he knew it would be pointless at this hour. By now she would be in bed asleep. So he would not see her until he returned to Gaspard, and knew that when she learned where he had gone, as inevitably she must, and why, it would seem to make him, in her eyes, a liar. Dully he had to face the probability that his private hopes in coming to this place had been all but dashed.

11

THEY were well mounted and armed, all five, moving along steadily in early-morning darkness, Macken, Gowan, Collis, Sloane and the man from the Treasury, Dillon.

Though it was not obvious, all were carrying heavy pistols except for Dillon. Macken's two deputies also had .44 Winchester rifles in saddle-scabbards, while Dillon's horse was carrying in a large canvas scabbard a Stevens 10-gauge single-barrel, the only kind of weapon Dillon had admitted to them that he had ever handled. All were wearing long, buff-coloured linen dusters and wide-brimmed hats of various vintages, Dillon's, however, a new, very stiff pale-grey one.

For Gowan, close-mouthed and thoughtful today, this posse was both like and unlike the one he had led hopefully out of Warbeck to investigate a report of deaths at a waylaid train and of the robbery that had taken place within the borders of Slane County; unlike, because Gowan had not at that time enjoyed the luxury of two deputies to ride along with him, and yet another to man the county office in his absence; like, because this group also had at least one element unaccustomed to this particular kind of work. Dillon.

There was no doubt at all in Gowan's mind that now they were actually on the journey, the Treasury man was uncomfortable, yet by the attitude of him, determined at this stage to see the matter through.

Macken, bobbing along in the lead, man and horse a greyish shape in this hour of early morning, his mind ranging ahead, believed that his present direction was probably about right, certainly right for an eventual approach through some valley of the Fayettes into that long, ancient canyon of the

High Torres known as Black Canyon, and, if his luck ran well, might also fetch him to the camp where Nash and his men might still be. But it would need to be daylight before he could be sure of that, and it depended largely on whether or not Nash still had a fire burning.

Weaving in and out between brush on the flats, leather creaking, bit-chains clinking, Sloane coughing from time to time, going now through the increasing pearly light of a new day, they arrived at a place where the ground sloped away very gradually, rock-strewn, and flattened out again until it touched the folded edges of the Fayettes. Here, Macken, more visible now in outline to those riding behind, held up one hand and the horses all came to a blowing, clinking halt, stiff riders muttering to them.

Gowan then took the opportunity to move slowly up alongside Macken and stopped again without exchanging a word as they allowed their eyes to traverse first in one direction, then all the way back again.

At a slight sound Macken turned his head to observe Collis dipping inside his duster to produce the makings. Macken said quietly, "Strike a match, Coll, an' I'll set yuh afoot without your goddamn boots."

Slowly Collis replaced the sack of tobacco. Dillon turned his cadaverous face towards Collis, perhaps to see if there was to be any reaction, but said nothing and looked to his front again.

When the light grew slightly stronger and they were all still quietly sitting their ear-flicking horses, Gowan, in a low voice, suddenly said, "There."

It was only a silk-thin tendril of smoke standing up from a cluster of large rocks some four hundred yards away, with more rocks and brush in between, as they could perceive from this very slightly elevated position.

Macken spoke in a hushed tone, turning his head towards the others. "Listen to me, Coll, Sloaney, rifles. Mr

Dillon, load the 10-gauge now, close it an' carry it in one hand. Be sure yuh got more cartridges where they're easy to git at. All dismount here an' picket the horses. We'll go in afoot, me on the left, then you, Mr Dillon, then Bob on your right, line-abreast. Sloaney an' Coll, keep enough of a distance back so yuh kin see us most o' the time. You're there fer cover in case it all shits on us, or they come out real fast, mounted. All clear?" No-one asked any questions. "Then let's git down an' git on with it."

The fire should not have had any life in it for someone had kicked dirt over it, but a few embers had remained, to be fanned by the gentlest of air movements, and one or two small scraps of dry brush had caught hold and that was why a wisp of smoke had been discernible from a distance.

Nothing else there was alive.

A dead man was lying, knees tucked up, a bullet-hole high up in his left side, a man of medium build, bony and coarse-skinned and whose stringy neck bore on its left side what was obviously an old rope-burn, a memento of some mysterious and unsuccessful lynching-party. The remains, so Collis maintained, were those of a man who had come with Nash, and whose name, so he had learned, was Staples. It had meant nothing to Collis at the time and meant nothing to either Macken or Gowan now. No attempt had been made to bury this man; his companions had simply ridden away, leaving him where he had fallen, prey to all scavengers.

No attempt had been made to bury Allie Joubert either, or even to cover her nakedness.

Part of her skull with its rich mass of brown, gold-shot hair had been blown away onto the ground with a shot which had been fired from close up, and the result was a coagulated, glutinous mess, moving with flies. Yet it was not only that sight which now caused Dillon to turn his long face away for several moments, but the sight, too, of her grossly blistered and hair-singed vagina, the result of unspeakable work there with a hot iron of some kind.

"Jesus Christ!" Collis said, his round face drained of colour, his head bowed.

Sloane's dust-reddened eyes turned to Dillon. "They sure did want to know real bad an' real quick where your goddamn' money had got to, mister."

"Nobody," Macken said after a moment, "nobody on God's earth deserves to die like that." A small silence fell. Then, "We'll lose some time we can't rightly afford to lose, but we'll set to, now, an' gather stones enough to cover 'em. Both of 'em."

Allie's ripped and soiled clothing lay on the ground all about, where they had torn it from her and dropped it. Sloane walked around slowly, gathering it all up, and when he had done so, spread it over her body. After that he set off to go back to the horses and bring them all in.

If there had been only sporadic talk between them from leaving Gaspard to observing Nash's night-camp, there was virtually none after they rode out of that camp and headed on up through a wide valley towards the canyon-split High Torres, what exchanges there were being mainly by brief looks and gestures. The scene they had come upon and the stone cairns they had left behind them had cast a pall over the entire party. Allie Joubert had been a compellingly attractive woman in the prime of her life, and there were those riding here who had cast their share of envious glances at Stace Culley who had been so frequently seen in her company.

Of the men in this posse, however, Gowan had had the closest contact with her, that, of course, while she had still been in Warbeck, and although it had turned out that right from the start she had been firmly of the Chandler camp, and probably had lent direct help to Jack Chandler after he had been let out of the cage, and certainly had offered him succour between the moment he had been shot and his ultimate death — and that right under Gowan's nose — even Gowan still could not bring himself to vilify the woman's memory. Perhaps her own truly horrifying end, the nature of which they had all seen, had somehow balanced all of that. Vaguely Gowan now wondered if he himself might have been prey to that strange magnetism she had had; but immediately he blinked that notion way, and instead, occupied himself by sombrely reviewing the long list of those who had now come to their deaths because of the robbery of the S-W freight: Stagg shot dead at the train, and at that same place five marshals shot, and the train's crew of five. Then in Warbeck Jack Chandler and his brother Ord, Pearce and the elder Nash, the young posseman, Billy Philips and the deputy, Augie Telfer. And now this man nobody seemed to have heard of, Staples, and of course

Allie Joubert. Nineteen. And Gowan had no doubt at all that if they did come up with Nash and the men with him, there would be others to bury before it was all done with. Wryly Gowan wondered if he might be one of them, and if that were to be the case, would Marion, after a suitable time of grieving, be just as content to be shut of him for good and all? No more letters, no more visits, no more unwanted overtures. Freedom. Gowan had left a message with a night-clerk at the Gaspard House but now wondered if it might have been better had he simply ridden away without saying anything, since not nearly enough could be conveyed in one short, hurried note. And even that had had a white lie in it. *Macken needs some help*. Gowan had thought of adding and underscoring the comment that it was nothing at all to do with recovering the money but at least he had thought better of that.

Presently Macken, leading by a dozen yards as was his custom, extended one of his arms and they all saw that he was pointing towards the blue-black entrance to the high-walled canyon which was their objective, a place which would dwarf the men and horses the moment they ventured inside. Now they were jouncing along at a steady pace, still quiet, each man with his own thoughts and if the truth were known, his own fears. If the men they sought were still in there, then for any or all of this party out of Gaspard, the minutes that were ticking by right now could well be measuring out the final hour of life.

12

IN single file, Macken, then Gowan, Collis and Sloane and finally Dillon began their entry into Black Canyon in clouded, still milky daylight, a light which appeared to be more subdued and challenged once they passed within the rearing walls of dark rock.

If there did exist an earthly gateway to Hell, Gowan thought, then it might well resemble this place, stark, overpowering in its very size, the wide, granular, sandy floor of it choked in places with hardy brush and humped and cluttered with the rockfalls of aeons, come down from the high canyon walls and otherwise undisturbed since the dawn of Time itself.

No doubt this would be a haunt of scuttling reptiles and of soaring eagles, highest and lowest living of the predators, and repository, perhaps, of the bleached remnants of the animals and of the men who once had ventured in here, never to emerge.

Collis, his round face turned upwards towards the bar of greyish light that seemed to be caught in a vice of obsidian rock, felt strangely diminished, a man who had left the known world and was entering a place in which meaningful measures of that outside world no longer had any relevance. As Sloane, riding behind him — and as perhaps all of them did — he felt physically reduced by this natural monstrosity which, because of the moving clouds high above it, seemed to be getting ready to crush him.

If Dillon, the city man, trailing them all, was prey to any of these new and uneasy sensations, his set-hard face was betraying nothing of them but his eyes were looking left and right as though seeking to strip the grey shadows from corners which, in Dillon's mind, might at any instant be torn by gunfire, and he was becoming increasingly uncomfortable over the way in which Macken, leading and now some forty-odd yards ahead of Dillon himself, was pressing on as though he had given those dangers no thought at all.

Macken in fact was far from sanguine about what he was doing, yet he had seen no point in hesitating for, if the sun should make an appearance through the cloud, slicing into this terrible place, probably at the day's zenith, Black Canyon must surely become an unliveable, fly-infested oven. Yet they would all sure need to keep a careful look-out. Therefore he glanced back again at those who were doggedly following him, horses nodding, shod hooves sometimes striking against stone, and called softly, "Colly, check up above an' to the left; Sloaney, the same to the right. Mr Dillon, keep a watch on our back-trail. Don't anybody let up. Drift off, an' the next second yuh could be dog-meat."

They went steadily on, holding their

horses to a quick trot, Collis and Sloane with rifles across crooked left arms, Dillon carrying the loaded and closed-up 10-gauge in his left hand, the butt-plate resting on his left thigh. All the riders were still wearing their long dusters, and Gowan, his hard eyes raking left, right and back again, and sighting sometimes beyond Macken's shoulder, thought that as the heat rose some outer clothing would have to be shed, for this, at least at the present time, was an enclosed, windless place.

By virtue of his six years of service in the county, Sloane considered himself senior of the deputies, and at this point, even while scouring with his narrowed, worried eyes the stark wall of the canyon rearing up across to his right, and the jumble of large rocks on the floor below it, allowed himself to wonder again about the man riding behind him, the official from the Treasury, Dillon. Dillon would be focusing his interest here solely on the money and the recovery of it. But if they did encounter Nash and it did come down to an ugly kind of shoot, what Dillon might do if such a fight should develop was what was chiefly concerning Sloane at this stage. When he glanced back over his shoulder, however, it was to see Dillon watching their back-trail as Macken had told him to do.

If those following had begun to believe that Macken would continue on at this steady pace until perhaps shot at, he gave the lie to that right now by holding up one hand and half turning his head. "Wait here!"

Gowan continued on for several yards and reined in beside him, the others closing up too, horses blowing, tossing heads.

"Up ahead between them two rocks there," Macken said, "I think I seen somethin'. We'll git down here, then me an' Bob, we'll go on in closer, afoot. Picket these animals where they stand. Mr Dillon, stay with 'em. You two work out to the sides with the rifles. Could be all on an' hootin' right soon, so go careful an' keep the yap down."

Some ten minutes later, Macken and Bob Gowan, having gone off quietly, came walking back, pistols still in hand, to where Dillon was waiting with the picketed horses, and they were soon rejoined by Sloane and Collis.

"Is it them?" Sloane asked, his pronounced Adam's apple working.

"By the time we got there, nobody was around," said Macken, "but somebody's here. Plenty o' tracks an' horse-apples an' some bootmarks. So, yeah, Nash. Question is, where the hell's he got to?"

Gowan had begun to have a very bad feeling about this enterprise, about this grim place, about the fact that they had managed to get as far as they had without being challenged; which by no means meant that they had not been seen.

Sloane glanced up at the moving sky, the clouds now showing definite signs of breaking up. "We're gonna be on a griddle in here afore long," he said.

Gowan then offered an opinion that when next they moved they might be wise to spread out some, even though there might be some disadvantage in that because of the great rocks that were so abundant — many as big as a Kansas barn — they would not all be visible to each other all of the time. Gowan did not wish to usurp Macken's authority over this posse but he did have a lawman's concerns about the wisdom of moving as a bunched-up party. Baldly — though he held back from saying it — if there was to be an ambush, then one of their number dropped was preferable to a group, a bigger target, all trying to get into cover at the same time.

To Gowan's relief, therefore, Macken said, "That sure makes a lot o' sense, Bob. An' maybe we'd be wiser to go forward from here afoot, leadin' the mounts. We don't want to leave 'em where some bastard might git at 'em."

Macken seemed now to be reverting to his more familiar persona, a cautious man adopting a prudent course. *Never assume anything.* It was perhaps a deliberately public withdrawal from the determined attitude which had brought them into the canyon quite boldly, driven too urgently by notions of retribution, for he and all of them had experienced first horror, then cold anger when they had found what had been left of Allie Joubert. Not only had she been bestially used but had then been flung aside like garbage, to rot.

"Might it be assumed," Dillon suggested, "that they have found the cave? There *was* said to be a cave?"

"It's more'n likely," Macken said.

"Then having perhaps located the money," said Dillon, "they must also show themselves in leaving this canyon. If we take up positions and wait for them, that could be our best chance to get our hands on it."

"If we kin still see 'em," said Macken. "If, by then, there's still enough daylight. An' in a night-shoot yuh can't be sure who's who."

That had the effect of shutting Dillon up, but what he had said seemed to reinforce their belief that his focus was still on the money, the Treasury money, *his* money as he might have come to view it. Possibly he had even lost sight of the dangers in confronting those men in order to get hold of it.

Some ten minutes later, Gowan having come to a halt, standing at the head of his bay horse, he waited for Macken to come clumping into view again on his right, then immediately made a hand signal.

From that moment on, as each man, leading his horse, reappeared, having been moving among the dwarfing rocks, the same signal was passed, and as they came walking to a common point, Gowan said, "There's some horses picketed up there near the wall of the canyon, about fifty, sixty yards."

One by one they came across to where Gowan was standing to take a look for themselves. True, there were several horses close together, standing quietly. But it was what was to be seen beyond them by a matter of another twenty yards which seized their interest.

There the dark rock of the canyon's side was cleft with a deeper darkness marking a very large fissure, but it was impossible to guess the extent of it or what lay behind it. A passage to nowhere? The opening to some cavern?

Finally Macken said, "That's got to be it."

"Let's git these mounts well out o' sight," Collis said, and they began shuffling the animals away, trying to be quiet about it but only partially succeeding.

Macken and Gowan, however, handing their horses to others, stood where they were for the purpose of studying what was before them.

"The only wide-open place we come to an' it's slap in front o' where these bastards are at. Too open, Bob, too open."

Gowan nodded. It was true that their view of the picketed horses and the entry to the passage or cave or whatever it was, was not obscured by the kind of huge rocks so evident elsewhere. Gowan then said, "It's also too damn' quiet. What if we did go forward an' got across to that cut an' they weren't in there, they were in among rocks an' brush behind us?"

Macken drew in a breath that filled his cheeks, then let it out slowly, and nodded. "Yeah, we'll sure not go at this bull-headed. We'll circle around among these rocks, make damn' sure Nash ain't waitin' out here to spring the trap."

Gowan, after glancing over his shoulder, asked in a lowered voice, "Dillon?"

Macken gave him a wintry grin and muttered, "Now we got as close as this to his goddamn sacks of money he'll not be satisfied to watch the horses no more." Then, "I wonder if the prick *is* any good with that 10-gauge."

As far as Gowan was concerned it was an unanswerable question, but the very presence of anyone unused to this kind of work was still nagging at him.

Both of them then moved away to join Dillon and the deputies waiting near the horses to tell them what was to be done. It was difficult to judge whether Dillon was pleased or not when Macken revealed that he would not be required to stay back to watch over the horses; but if the testing conditions and the increasing tensions were beginning to affect him, he did not show that either, though his usually barber-clean face was now stubbled with whiskers and there were dark sacks under his eyes.

Neither Sloane nor Collis had much to say now, for it was clear to all that the next ten minutes could turn out to be the last they would ever know on earth, and perhaps each man, irrespective of who he was or what he was, might be thinking — even silently addressing some deity unspecified — "*If it comes, make it clean and quick.*" If such individual introspection was indeed the case, then for at least one among them it was a wish not to be fulfilled.

Seven minutes later the truth of their earlier conjecture about whether the men they sought were inside a cave or outside, hidden among the rocks, was discovered to be a mixture of both. Some were inside, at least one outside; but this did not become apparent until, separated again, they had made some inroads into searching this whole rock-cluttered, brush area.

Sloane was the first of them to get into trouble and because, as had been the case a little earlier, each was sometimes hidden not only from those farthest from him but from the nearest man, he was in a sense isolated at the time as well as being in the wrong place.

As far as Macken and Gowan, the longest distance from him, were

concerned, Sloane, carrying his rifle
— as was Collis — must have seen
something threatening only at the last
instant, for they heard his voice call out
something indistinguishable and right
on top of that there came gunfire; only
a single shot, and without doubt from
a pistol.

As one, Macken and Gowan, at the
time within sight of one another, went
down on one knee, though some forty
feet separated them and they could not
of course see what was going on.

Collis, also unsighted, aware only of
Dillon across to his right, also stopped
in his tracks, holding his Winchester
in both hands and crouching slightly.
Dillon, with his 10-gauge, stopped also
and stood looking around him in a
rather bemused fashion.

"Git down!" Collis yelled. Dillon fell
to his knees as though he had been
bludgeoned.

By now Sloane was in all sorts of
bother. He had been shot at by some
bastard who was lying on the flattish

top of one of the most substantial rocks hereabouts, and while he had not been hit, Sloane had obeyed a natural impulse to get the hell out of the way, which in his particular situation meant going quickly to his left. While he was getting it done he was shot at again by the same man, dust jumping alarmingly right where Sloane had been only a moment earlier; and though he must now be out of sight of the shooter, the second shot had had the effect of prompting him to run more quickly and much further than he might otherwise have done. Thus Sloane suddenly found himself out in part of that open space which had been adjudged by both Macken and Gowan to be very dangerous indeed.

Again a shot erupted from that same elevated place but went singing a long way above Sloane's head and was indeed fired by a man who could no longer even see his target; and much too late, Sloane realized that he had allowed himself to be kind of herded away from immediate danger towards this place that seemed deserted but which was much more hazardous.

From the obsidian gash in the canyon's wall came a lashing rifle-shot, a sound that went bouncing away again and again off granite faces, and this time Sloane was hit fair and square, and still running, cartwheeled when the first bullet took him, his own rifle, at the moment of impact, involuntarily cast away, his hat coming off as Sloane struck the ground hard and went rolling, the long linen duster he was wearing making him seem even more awkward as he went down.

The spot where he had been dropped was almost half way from where Gowan and very soon Macken were now observing from the jutting corner of a house-sized chunk of stone, and the deadly entrance to the cave.

The horses belonging to the Nash party were acting up now, pulling at their picket-pins, whickering, eyes rolling.

Sloane was not dead.

Macken's instinct was to break cover and go to the man's aid but he had abandoned any notion of that before a second rifle-shot lashed out and stone chips flew only a foot from Macken's head, causing him to jerk back out of sight.

Gowan, also withdrawing to safety, now remarked that they would have to get this Goddamn' mess sorted out fast.

Well out of view of that scene, Dillon was still kneeling, but now he saw the other deputy, Collis, coming edging back towards him holding a rifle and with nodding, jerking head-signs trying to convey to Dillon that there had to be a shooter lying somewhere on top of one of the rocks up ahead of them. Dillon did not seem to understand at once, so Collis had to come close enough to explain it to him.

"What can we do?" Dillon asked.

"Ain't real sure," said Collis, "but there's a rise in the ground over yonder where that brush is, an' them stepped-up rocks. I'm gonna work up that way an' see if I kin git a shot at the bastard if he's still there."

"Do you think he actually shot anybody?" asked Dillon.

"Mebbe, mebbe not. What I do reckon is this. Your best move is to git your carcase across to where Macken's at an' tell him what I'm gonna be up to, an' then stay real close to him." Clearly Collis had no great faith in this Dillon of the town suits in the kind of crisis they were now facing. And surprisingly, the man from the Treasury, the man accustomed when among his own kind to exerting an often despotic command, now, as he had done earlier at Macken's behest, moved at once to obey this unwashed, smelly, fat-faced and none-too-savoury-looking lawman.

Sloane was very badly hurt and in fact in great pain, the tangled long duster now looking more like a bloodied shroud. What had begun as a deep moaning sound coming from him had now become a higher-pitched and demonic noise of almost rythmic insistence; an intake of rattling breath then a shrieking explosion of sound that soon began to grate on both Macken and Gowan who from time to time risked taking a look out towards Sloane.

The shot man was making movements too, but little more than boot-scuffing twitches which in his semiconscious, tortured awareness probably seemed to be movements of a more gainful kind.

At other sounds, as one they spun around.

Dillon came crouching — though in his case there seemed scarcely a need to crouch — carrying the 10-gauge and breathlessly delivering Collis's message.

Soon it was Dillon, sweating uncomfortably and out of sorts, who was the most disturbed by the noises that were coming from Sloane.

"My God, Macken, isn't there something we can do for the man?"

"Not for the present," Macken said. "He's too far away an' they're well holed up across there, with a rifle on him. Anybody tryin' to git to him wouldn't step five paces."

Sloane, screaming, was also trying to shout something but it was incomprehensible.

"Oh, my God!" Dillon was looking desperately from one to the other. Suddenly he straightened up and went a few awkward steps away from them, leaving the shotgun on the ground, and began vomiting.

Collis, having divested himself of his long duster, had managed to inch his way up the broken, sloping ground, moving close to clawing brush, sometimes being raked by it, easing the Winchester ahead of him. So far it had been a slow, uncomfortable crawl but now he came to what was the lowest of the three stepped-up slabs of ancient rock, and he now set about climbing onto it, and once there, pulling up onto the next, until at last he found himself, bruised, scored and sweating, on the topmost one.

From here he found he could get at least a partial view of the canyon's littered floor, but most important of all, could now glimpse the place from which the earlier shooting had come.

Collis's pulses gave a surge when he realized that he had actually got it worked out right. There, some eighty feet to his left and slightly ahead of where he now was, on what was a very large, almost flat-topped chunk of weather-ravaged rock where there would have been enough space to assemble all of the Saturday night customers of the Red Deuce, lay one man, armed, as far as Collis could see, with a long-barrelled pistol but no rifle.

In his concentration Collis's tongue was pushing one of his cheeks out as he palmed one hand down and raised himself so that his left knee was stepped up. He then placed his left elbow on his left thigh and brought the stock of the Winchester firmly into his right shoulder, pulling it down from the top so that his clothing would bunch beneath it and hold it steady. Now he was fully exposed but also had a clear view of the prone man who, at this particular moment, was looking the other way.

Some stirring of an extra sense, however, must have sent this man a warning, for as Collis was lining him up, his head turned sharply and he saw what was about to happen. This man, Collis thought, now that he had got a better look at him, was the one named Bascom.

Bascom — for he indeed it was — lost no time in letting loose a smoky grey stab of shot at Collis, and then went rolling away fast, no doubt to disturb Collis's aim. Bascom's lead from his hurried, reflex shot, not surprisingly, went nowhere near the rifleman, for it had been the product of sudden, sweating panic. Yet three more times now Bascom fired, the detonations magnified by the hard canyon, but Collis was aware of the low-humming passage of only one of the slugs. There had been three shots earlier, so if he had not already done so, Bascom would have to reload to try again or get out of sight quickly.

Retreating from Collis's threat was the option that Bascom took, but clearly a descent from the massive rock he was on was not an operation that could be rushed. The thing was all of forty feet high and the floor of the canyon surrounding it had a dangerously broken surface. A fall from near the top would possibly be fatal. So Bascom began ducking here and there, unnerved now until, looking again across the void which separated them he again saw the calm deliberation of Collis, still at the half-kneel, sighting the rifle on him afresh.

Bascom's nerve snapped. Half crouching, he began backing away, empty pistol in one hand, the other raised, palm towards Collis, as though imploring him to wait, to desist, to give a man quarter.

But Collis's mind was still filled with the seared, ravaged, once-lovely body of Allie Joubert and he wondered if Bascom had held one of her legs while someone else, Nash most likely, went at her with his terrible iron.

Bascom's yell was near to a scream, half plea, half command, the man still backing away in the same strange, hand-raised, crouching fashion. "No! No! Fer God's sake!"

The cutting lash of Collis's rifle went splashing far up the jagged canyon. Bascom, already going backwards, was punched harder back one, two steps, the second one into space, and after seeming to hang there a moment, vanished from Collis's view.

Collis worked the lever of the rifle, ejecting, reloading, then began making his purposeful way back down the route he had come up. Somewhere off in the direction of Macken and the others he could hear some strange, persistent, high-pitched sound, this having followed a rifle-shot across there. Picking his way down, Collis was now wondering where Sloane could have got to.

Dillon, his gritty eyes now wide, his long face haggard, also gave the impression that he was all but pressing his hands over his ears, such were the appalling, tortured sounds coming from Sloane; but Dillon was no longer saying anything about it, for Macken had left him in no doubt at all that for any one of them to venture out into the open would be to invite death.

Then when Gowan, risking a glance, said to Macken, "Look", Dillon's attention was drawn, also, and it was to see Sloane, encumbered by the long duster, still in deep agony, actually trying to crawl, perhaps attempting to get away from his appalling pain.

Then something within the Treasury man simply snapped. A man well out of his own element, was Dillon, here in this awful, so aptly-named place of sombre, rearing rock, of dust and brush and the smell of heat and dung and the sounds of echoing gunfire, and the terrifying noises, not in the least like any human noises he had heard, coming from the posseman who had been shot.

Goaded beyond threat and fear by all of this, perhaps too by a sense of his own impotence and horror and rage, Dillon, carrying his 10-guage in both his pale hands suddenly ran past Macken, while Gowan, trying to seize hold of him, missed the grab and half feel in his wake, cursing.

Macken yelled, "No!" but Dillon had already gone from the sheltering rock and was out in the open.

Gowan shouted, "Cover!" and both he and Macken also went out quickly and with deliberate measured movement, began shooting their pistols towards the dark cleft in the rock opposite.

And Dillon, having now got as far as the twitching, bawling lump that was Sloane, Dillon's stiff-brimmed, just-so hat gone, tall in his long buff duster, shotgun up, let fly towards the cave with a smoky, jolting, wad-spurting thump of a shot, then dropped the shot-gun, stooped and, raising Sloane by his upper arms, began moving backwards step by straining step towards the safety of the rock he had lately left.

Gowan, though roundly cursing the man's insanity, was starting towards them when a rifle-bullet whacked Dillon and drove him back, though he was still firmly gripping Sloane; then a second bullet sent reddish spray flying from Dillon's head and now he was detached from Sloane and down and rolling in dust and blood. Another bullet punched Sloane and put him beyond all further pain.

Gowan and Macken — who had also started forward — now hurling themselves back towards the salvation of the rock, also hit the dirt, rolling, lethally-searching bullets ripping the ground behind them. Then both were back in, lying sweating, chests heaving, as Collis arrived from the opposite direction wanting to know what in the name of God was going on.

"It's all turned to goddamn' shit," Macken said, "an' now we got ourselves two spare horses."

Gowan had been gauging his chances of getting to the Nash mounts, reasoning that if he were to circle back and approach them by staying close in to the wall of the canyon, there was a chance he might do it through the tightening of the angle of sight for those standing just inside the cave, and he said as much to Macken and Collis now. Yet hardly had he put the proposition than Collis, stepping to one side and looking beyond Gowan's shoulder, yelled, "They're out!"

Gowan and Macken spun around, both dropping to one knee, while Collis was bringing his Winchester up.

Nash and Brophy it was, the survivors; only two, certainly, but no less menacing for that, even though only one, Brophy, had a rifle; running hard from the cave towards their picketed animals, only a matter of twenty yards or so, yet a hell of a long way in view of Collis's rifle which by now they would have seen.

In the event though, Brophy outthought Collis, smashing a shot away from his own rifle as he ran; no attempt at aiming, little chance of being rewarded with a hit, but Brophy shrewd enough to know that a rifle discharged within effective range, even if not well-aimed, will cause those who are even minimally at risk to go ducking away instinctively.

In that purchased tick of time, Nash and Brophy arrived on the far side of the picketed horses.

"They're there," Collis muttered. "They got us flat-footed an' now they'll pull out fer good."

"Don't reckon so," said Macken. "They ain't got what they come fer, an' Nash, he won't leave without it."

And doubtless they would be banking on the possemen not trying to kill the horses in an effort to expose the men who were behind them; so they would use some of the mounts as shields in order to move around, perhaps even to separate. And this was exactly what occurred. One of them, Nash so they thought, began running with one of the horses, moving quickly, screened by the animal's shoulder, while the rifleman, Brophy, also headed away with a horse, but in the opposite direction, towards the canyon's mouth.

At one and the same time, Macken and Gowan realized the implications of that and Macken spun around to Collis. "Track that shit there with your rifle, afore he gits to where our mounts is at."

Without a moment's hesitation, weaving in and out between high rocks, his thonged hat bouncing between his shoulders, Collis went jogging away.

Nash, with the other horse, was by now almost across the open space and in among rocks and brush at the farther side, clearly not wishing to get himself trapped inside the cave, money or no money.

Macken made an arm motion to Gowan who at once set off after Nash, while Macken himself headed for the black maw of the cave.

By now, however, Nash had gone from sight. Gowan, slowing came walking down to a stop, shucked the long duster, then went jogging on. After the shooting and all the movement, an uneasy quiet had fallen.

Nash, up on the horse, came bursting from cover, crouching in the saddle, furious at being thwarted at the last hour, seeking now to crush any of these men who had come out of nowhere; furious too, no doubt, that Culley, whom they had hit at the night-camp, but carelessly lost track of, had apparently not died, but having heard too much had lived to send a posse to this canyon.

Gowan, exposed to a charging, mounted man, turned and ran, crouching, hearing the swiftly-closing horse at his back. Nash must have believed that here was his great moment, when he could easily reduce the odds by one, out of a posse that must have come in short-handed to start with, and had included one fool who had been dead meat from the moment he had come blundering out to help another who had been dropped, gut-shot, out in the open.

Gowan reached the duster that he had shucked off, seized it and turning, whirled the large, flapping garment above his head, the running horse now only yards away. Eyes whitening, the animal tried to veer sharply, the rider now wrestling to control it, and as it went thundering by, Gowan, on one knee, close enough to smell the horse, covered in the dust it was raising, blasted his pistol.

Nash went riding on. Gowan fired again, swathed in dust and gunsmoke, then could no longer see clearly, shaking his head, brushing a sweat-soaked sleeve across eyes that were afire with grit. The next thing he was aware of was Macken's voice.

"Yuh hit the bastard! Yuh hit 'im, Bob!"

Looming through the swirling dust, Macken, long pistol in his hand, joined Gowan and they both were both looking in the direction the horseman had taken.

Brophy could not have failed to hear the echoing shots that Gowan had fired but he was now within sight of Macken's horses and knew that if he could just get to them and succeed in running them off, then this bastard and what was left of his posse would have more problems than he was going to be able to handle. Rifle in one hand, he had just pulled the first of the picket-pins when Collis, forty yards away, propped against an upthrust of granite, having waited patiently until Brophy straightened and stood away a moment, no horse behind him, shot him in the head, blowing part of his skull away in a spray of blood and glutinous matter, setting Brophy's horse and the freed horse prancing away and sending Brophy pitching down and over, falling beneath one of the still-picketed horses, causing it to go blowing and pulling and skitter-stepping in a semicircle.

When Macken and Gowan came jogging into view, Macken now hatless, Gowan, like Collis, with his shallow-crowned black hat hanging at his back, the man with the rifle asked, "Where's Nash?"

Breathing hard, Macken said, "Nash? Fell off his horse with Bob's lead in him." Then: "Go git them loose animals."

"Twenty-four," Gowan murmured.

"What?" asked Macken.

"Dead," said Gowan. "Twenty-four dead, with Nash an' this rooster here. All for the money. Even Dillon."

"Well, in the finish," Macken observed, "it did seem to slip his mind."

Gowan nodded. He did not even begin to understand that either.

236

"C'mon," he said, "we'd best go back an' take a look, find out if the stuff *is* in there." Gowan was mildly surprised to discover that he no longer much cared whether the money was there or not. In some ways he even hoped that it might not be. What he ached for now was to be back in Gaspard, hoping to God that Marion was still there. Once before, when he had been occupied elsewhere, she had slipped away from him.

"What's up?" Macken asked.

Gowan looked at him, shook his head briefly, then trudged on by. Collis was engaged with the loose horses.

Soberly Macken studied the slightly stooped back of the dusty man walking away, then began following him, a pair of slow-moving ants in the vast, overwhelming gloom of that benighted place. Macken suddenly felt very old indeed.

FIGHTING RAMROD
Charles N. Heckelmann

Most men would have cut their losses, but Frazer counted the bullets in his guns and said he'd soak the range in blood before he'd give up another inch of what was his.

LONE GUN
Eric Allen

Smoke Blackbird had been away too long. The Lequires had seized the Blackbird farm, forcing the Indians and settlers off, and no one seemed willing to fight! He had to fight alone.

THE THIRD RIDER
Barry Cord

Mel Rawlins wasn't going to let anything stand in his way. His father was murdered, his two brothers gone. Now Mel rode for vengeance.

ARIZONA DRIFTERS
W. C. Tuttle

When drifting Dutton and Lonnie Steelman decide to become partners they find that they have a common enemy in the formidable Thurston brothers.

TOMBSTONE
Matt Braun

Wells Fargo paid Luke Starbuck to outgun the silver-thieving stagecoach gang at Tombstone. Before long Luke can see the only thing bearing fruit in this eldorado will be the gallows tree.

HIGH BORDER RIDERS
Lee Floren

Buckshot McKee and Tortilla Joe cut the trail of a border tough who was running Mexican beef into Texas. They stopped the smuggler in his tracks.

BRETT RANDALL, GAMBLER
E. B. Mann

Larry Day had the choice of running away from the law or of assuming a dead man's place. No matter what he decided he was bound to end up dead.

THE GUNSHARP
William R. Cox

The Eggerleys weren't very smart. They trained their sights on Will Carney and Arizona's biggest blood bath began.

THE DEPUTY OF SAN RIANO
Lawrence A. Keating and
Al. P. Nelson

When a man fell dead from his horse, Ed Grant was spotted riding away from the scene. The deputy sheriff rode out after him and came up against everything from gunfire to dynamite.

FARGO: MASSACRE RIVER
John Benteen

The ambushers up ahead had now blocked the road. Fargo's convoy was a jumble, a perfect target for the insurgents' weapons!

SUNDANCE: DEATH IN THE LAVA
John Benteen

The Modoc's captured the wagon train and its cargo of gold. But now the halfbreed they called Sundance was going after it . . .

HARSH RECKONING
Phil Ketchum

Five years of keeping himself alive in a brutal prison had made Brand tough and careless about who he gunned down . . .

FARGO: PANAMA GOLD
John Benteen

With foreign money behind him, Buckner was going to destroy the Panama Canal before it could be completed. Fargo's job was to stop Buckner.

FARGO:
THE SHARPSHOOTERS
John Benteen

The Canfield clan, thirty strong were raising hell in Texas. Fargo was tough enough to hold his own against the whole clan.

PISTOL LAW
Paul Evan Lehman

Lance Jones came back to Mustang for just one thing — revenge! Revenge on the people who had him thrown in jail.

HELL RIDERS
Steve Mensing

Wade Walker's kid brother, Duane, was locked up in the Silver City jail facing a rope at dawn. Wade was a ruthless outlaw, but he was smart, and he had vowed to have his brother out of jail before morning!

DESERT OF THE DAMNED
Nelson Nye

The law was after him for the murder of a marshal — a murder he didn't commit. Breen was after him for revenge — and Breen wouldn't stop at anything . . . blackmail, a frameup . . . or murder.

DAY OF THE COMANCHEROS
Steven C. Lawrence

Their very name struck terror into men's hearts — the Comancheros, a savage army of cutthroats who swept across Texas, leaving behind a bloodstained trail of robbery and murder.

SUNDANCE: SILENT ENEMY
John Benteen

A lone crazed Cheyenne was on a personal war path. They needed to pit one man against one crazed Indian. That man was Sundance.

LASSITER
Jack Slade

Lassiter wasn't the kind of man to listen to reason. Cross him once and he'll hold a grudge for years to come — if he let you live that long.

LAST STAGE TO GOMORRAH
Barry Cord

Jeff Carter, tough ex-riverboat gambler, now had himself a horse ranch that kept him free from gunfights and card games. Until Sturvesant of Wells Fargo showed up.

McALLISTER ON THE COMANCHE CROSSING
Matt Chisholm

The Comanche, McAllister owes them a life — and the trail is soaked with the blood of the men who had tried to outrun them before.

QUICK-TRIGGER COUNTRY
Clem Colt

Turkey Red hooked up with Curly Bill Graham's outlaw crew. But wholesale murder was out of Turk's line, so when range war flared he bucked the whole border gang alone . . .

CAMPAIGNING
Jim Miller

Ambushed on the Santa Fe trail, Sean Callahan is saved by two Indian strangers. But there'll be more lead and arrows flying before the band join Kit Carson against the Comanches.

GUNSLINGER'S RANGE
Jackson Cole

Three escaped convicts are out for revenge. They won't rest until they put a bullet through the head of the dirty snake who locked them behind bars.

RUSTLER'S TRAIL
Lee Floren

Jim Carlin knew he would have to stand up and fight because he had staked his claim right in the middle of Big Ike Outland's best grass.

THE TRUTH ABOUT SNAKE RIDGE
Marshall Grover

The troubleshooters came to San Cristobal to help the needy. For Larry and Stretch the turmoil began with a brawl and then an ambush.

WOLF DOG RANGE
Lee Floren

Will Ardery would stop at nothing, unless something stopped him first — like a bullet from Pete Manly's gun.

DEVIL'S DINERO
Marshall Grover

Plagued by remorse, a rich old reprobate hired the Texas Trouble-shooters to deliver a fortune in greenbacks to each of his victims.

GUNS OF FURY
Ernest Haycox

Dane Starr, alias Dan Smith, wanted to close the door on his past and hang up his guns, but people wouldn't let him.

DONOVAN
Elmer Kelton

Donovan was supposed to be dead. Uncle Joe Vickers had fired off both barrels of a shotgun into the vicious outlaw's face as he was escaping from jail. Now Uncle Joe had been shot — in just the same way.

CODE OF THE GUN
Gordon D. Shirreffs

MacLean came riding home, with saddle tramp written all over him, but sewn in his shirt-lining was an Arizona Ranger's star.

GAMBLER'S GUN LUCK
Brett Austen

Gamblers seldom live long. Parker was a hell of a gambler. It was his life — or his death . . .

ORPHAN'S PREFERRED
Jim Miller

Sean Callahan answers the call of the Pony Express and fights Indians and outlaws to get the mail through.

DAY OF THE BUZZARD
T. V. Olsen

All Val Penmark cared about was getting the men who killed his wife.

THE MANHUNTER
Gordon D. Shirreffs

Lee Kershaw knew that every Rurale in the territory was on the lookout for him. But the offer of $5,000 in gold to find five small pieces of leather was too good to turn down.